To Darlene,

Thanks for your
support &
enthusiasm.

Stay Green +
Sustainable.

Albie
&
Goner

# Facing the Drought

## A MUSICAL BOOK

THE EARTH IS WHAT WE ALL HAVE IN COMMON.

Library of Congress Control Number: 2016939343
ISBN: 978-0-9969753-0-8 (Hard copy)
ISBN: 978-0-9969753-1-5 (Paperback)
ISBN: 978-0-9969753-2-2 (eBook)
First Edition

To learn more about us, visit **www.thesupersustainables.com**

For questions and comments, email us at **thesupersustainables@gmail.com**

# THE SUPER SUSTAINABLES
## YOU CAN BE A HERO TOO

# Facing the Drought
## A MUSICAL BOOK

Story by Albin R. Gielicz & Gonen Yacov, with Shelley Sunjka

Illustrated by Gonen Yacov & Filipe Sabino

Designed by Gonen Yacov for GY Creative Studio

Songs

Lyrics by: Gonen Yacov, Ed Munter & James Harmon III

Music by: James Harmon III & Ed Munter for Masters of Now Productions

Produced by: Klim Ivanin, Ed Munter & James Harmon III

We are two community-minded, do-gooders living in Santa Monica, California who are committed to promoting environmental, social and economic sustainability in our city, state, country and world. We are a solid team with over 30 years of experience in marketing and design.

Together, we have created the Super Sustainables in order to realize our purpose to support a resource-smart generation of environmental heroes. The future depends on our ability and willingness to mitigate the impacts of climate change so that the earth can continue to support all life.

Therefore our book is dedicated to the children of today who are the leaders of tomorrow. May they grow to make more responsible and sustainable choices than their predecessors.

During the creation of this project, we were greatly inspired by these words from Abraham Lincoln:

*"A child is a person who is going to carry on what you have started.*
*He is going to sit where you are sitting,*
*And when you are gone,*
*Attend to those things which you think are important.*
*You may adopt all the policies you please,*
*But how they are carried out depends on him.*
*He will assume control of your cities, states and nations.*
*He is going to move in and take over your*
*Churches, schools, universities and corporations....*
*The fate of humanity is in his hands."*

With these powerful words come the responsibility to impart on our children the importance of living more sustainably, while respecting and preserving our beautiful earth for generations to come.

The Authors,
Albin and Gonen

# CONTENTS

Chapter 1

# Origins

### CRAAAAAAAAACK!

A great crevice opened up, and the ground shuddered, giving off a deep moan as tiny rivulets started streaming over the edges of the rock. The moan grew louder and louder, and the rivulets flowed in stronger streams until water gushed into the cracks, with shudders coming at regular intervals.

Earth was being abused, and the crevice was her aching heart...

As the hole grew bigger, the magnetic forces and electrical currents deep below her surface swirled together, forming a powerful, glowing energy that balled itself into a spinning silver orb. As the energy became stronger, a dazzling blast of light burst upward, whirling toward the surface more quickly than a tornado. It spun and spun, growing larger by the moment, pulling rocks and bits of plant and earth into its depths. When it reached the surface, the revolutions sputtered, as though they were beginning to break.

The cyclone slowed, then sped up again, its winds becoming higher and louder.

Then, as if it suddenly remembered what it was meant to be doing, the storm stopped completely. The debris it had collected fell to the ground, and the walls of mist and light fell with it.

When the air had cleared and silence once again reigned, one thing remained behind. A beautiful, glowing woman with a curtain of silvery white hair hanging down to her waist stood where the tornado had once raged. She wore a long, white dress and had eyes of the brightest green.

She was, she realized, the only representative of Earth who could take human form in times of great need. And if she was here…it meant Earth had great need for her help.

• • • •

The mystical woman in white made her way over to the huge, gaping hole, shocked and deeply saddened at what she saw.

"Mother Nature," cried Earth. "I have summoned you because I desperately need your help. I fear I will be damaged beyond repair by the irresponsible humans who live in the world today. They just don't care how they hurt and abuse me anymore!"

Mother Nature looked at the troubled land surrounding her and shook her head. She saw that Earth was correct—the ground strewn with litter, the sky gray with pollution. She closed her eyes and breathed deeply, sending her thoughts into the body of the ground from which she'd been born. She realized the world itself was suffering. The waters were unhealthy, the land was dying, and the air itself was so impure she could hardly breathe.

"Yes," she answered. "Things are worse than the last time I saw the surface. I will go into the human world and teach them to take better care of their home."

"Thank you," said Earth. "I fear that if we don't do something soon, it will be too late to save me, and the humans who depend on me in the future will be in trouble!"

"I'll be back as soon as I can," said Mother Nature. She spun around, whipping her hair, and shot off in a blaze of light.

She soared high above the earth, weaving between the clouds, and was horrified at what she saw. All over the world, people didn't seem to care about the beautiful earth anymore. Mother Nature saw littering, oil spills, air and water pollution, mountains of trash piling up, and ongoing droughts—all products of humanity's way of life. As she passed over factories belching toxic fumes from their chimneys, her eyes burned and her throat constricted as she coughed and choked from the smoke. Her heart nearly broke as she saw children sickened by pollution, animals gunned down by poachers, and huge barren tracts of land where beautiful, lush, green forests had once grown.

Tears streamed down her face. Things were far worse than she had thought, and she realized she couldn't fix them by herself.

She needed help.

# Origins

She paused, found a cloud that would support her, and floated there, trying to think of a plan. There had to be a way—a way to reach humanity, a way to get them to listen. To make them understand they were endangering not just their world, but also their very existence.

But how?

She was starting to despair she couldn't help after all, when suddenly an idea flew into her head.

"That's it!" she said excitedly, and bounced off the cloud, shooting through the air faster than a bolt of lightning. She arrived back at the center of the earth moments later, breathless and full of hope.

She looked at Earth with kind eyes. "You were right," she said. "Things are bad out there, but I have a plan to save you. We have to change how humans behave. I can't do it alone, though. I'm going to need a bit of help."

"Help?" asked Earth, her voice shocked. "Who could possibly help me more than you?"

"All life on earth depends on four elements: Earth, Air, Fire and Water," Mother Nature began. "Without them, there is nothing. These four elements will help me." She smiled, very pleased with herself, but quickly realized Earth didn't understand.

"I don't see how you are going to get those elements to help you," Earth answered slowly. "They don't have a body or a mind."

"That's just it," Mother Nature replied. "I'm going to give them both! I don't know why I didn't think of it before," she continued, suddenly remembering her role as Mother Nature. "You see, 4.5 billion years ago when the world was created, as the mother of all natural phenomena, I was entrusted with the spirits of the four elements that form the foundation of our existence. I carry their spirits here with me wherever I go." She put her hands over her heart, feeling the elements there, and knowing they were willing—and ready—to help her save the world.

Raising her hand to touch the colorful jeweled necklace at her throat, she said, "Now it is time to release them. I'm going to set them free to help me. They are the elements, the power of four."

"And this will save us all?" Earth asked, the hope in her voice as clear as the song of rain against the trees.

MOTHER NATURE'S SONG
**THE POWER OF FOUR**

*PLAY* this song at
TheSuperSustainables.com

Mother Nature nodded. "Each of these four jewels holds the spirit of one of the elements," she continued. "The red jewel contains the spirit of fire, green the spirit of earth, blue the spirit of water, and purple the spirit of air. I will release them into the world, and they will give me the help I need. They will find the people I need. I will place these spirits into four very special individuals. In their human forms, they will communicate with others and encourage them to change their behavior."

"Thank you," said Earth, finally understanding.

Mother Nature simply nodded and began to gently rub each jewel, whispering as she did.

*Fire, Water, Earth, and Air,*
*Help me save the earth from those who don't care.*
*Let's help the world in her hour of need,*
*Off we go with patience, wisdom, and speed.*
*We must find special ones who care for our plight,*
*And use all their powers in our Earth's sad fight.*

Origins

*So go out there now, I will be there to guide you,*
*And find a way to teach those who don't have a clue.*
*Let's show them how to save the earth by choosing*
*careful actions,*
*Teaching them to treat the world with love, care,*
*and compassion.*
*You will now work as one, like never before,*
*You are the elements, the power of four.*

As she said the words, an orb emerged from each jewel. Each orb contained an element inside—a small flame, a beautiful leaf, crashing waves, and a small, whirling tornado. Mother Nature gathered them gently in her hands and took off in a flash of bright light, shouting down to Earth, "I'll be back soon!"

She soared above the earth for a while, seeking the best place to release the elements to fulfill their destiny. As she passed over

California, she saw four young women relaxing in Palisades Park, overlooking the beach in Santa Monica. They didn't know each other; in fact, each seemed caught up in her own thoughts and activities. But they had something in common: They were pregnant, a tiny bundle of life growing inside them.

"Perfect!" muttered Mother Nature. She released the orbs and sent them flying toward the women.

Instinctively, each element knew which one to pick, because the tiny life within each woman's belly spoke out to the appropriate element.

The first lady turned her face upward to enjoy the warmth of the fiery sun just as the fire element burst out of its orb and entered her body. As fire settled inside her, she felt her baby kick for the first time.

The lady near the edge of the cliff looking out at the sea felt a fine, misty spray from the ocean on her face as a huge wave broke and the water element entered her body. She, too, felt her baby kick for the first time.

A sudden gust of wind caused the third lady to grab her hat as a tiny tornado swirled around her. "Goodness, you are going to be an energetic child!" she exclaimed, hugging her tummy as her baby somersaulted inside her.

The earth element waited until last. A small tremor shook the park for three seconds while the element found its way into the last woman's body. The four mothers smiled at each other as they made their way out of the park to carry on with their day, completely unaware of the bond just created between them. Little did they know that, over the next few months, they would each give birth to an exceptionally gifted child who would grow to impact the world in a very special way.

Excited, Mother Nature smiled as she watched from above. Her plan had just begun!

Chapter 2

# Fifteen Years Later

# Arielle

"Oh, gross!" said Arielle as a drop of sweat from her face landed on her iPhone. She wiped the droplet off the screen and groaned inwardly as she examined the picture on it. *I can't put a picture up on Instagram with me looking like this*, she thought. She had been sitting outside, trying to quickly update her Instagram profile before cheerleading practice, but hadn't realized how hot it was.

Any picture right now would show her wilted, sweating, and sporting mascara smears. Not cool.

"Why is it so hot? What happened to winter?" she complained. "I'm already disgusting, and we haven't even started practice yet." She closed out of Instagram and glanced at the clock on the phone.

The heat wasn't her only problem. She was also *late*.

"No," she muttered, jumping to her feet and dashing toward the locker room. She couldn't afford to be late again—no amount of excuses about selfies would save her this time.

● ● ● ●

Arielle was almost done changing for practice. *No one's here yet,* she thought to herself, *so I guess more mirrors for me*. She stood in front of the full-length mirror in the locker room to make sure her uniform fit perfectly. Without thinking, she took a few steps back from the mirror for a better look and accidentally knocked her open backpack off the bench. As it hit the floor, everything spilled out and scattered.

"Oh, come on!" she said in frustration. "I can't even enjoy myself for five minutes." She bent over quickly to pick up Birdie, her stuffed toy bird, and said in a wondering voice, "what am I going to do about you? I mean, I'm like, still bringing you with me everywhere." She gave Birdie a tight squeeze.

She knew if anyone saw it, they'd tease her horribly for having it at school. Though she felt silly for still being so attached to it—at 14 years old—she couldn't bear the thought of anyone else saying so. Yet she also couldn't bear the thought of leaving it at home. She had made a few attempts to wean herself from her "friend" but never could. Birdie had been a present from her mom and dad on the day she was born, and they had been inseparable ever since. Deep down, she knew the day would come when she would have to let go of the small, soft, red bird, but she wasn't ready just yet. If she continued to be very careful, she felt sure nobody would discover her secret.

# Fifteen Years Later

Suddenly, Arielle heard someone calling her name. She nervously adjusted her uniform. "Oh no," she groaned, "I need to put you away before someone sees you." Arielle stuffed Birdie back into her bag, picked up the rest of her things from the floor, quickly shoved her bag into her locker, and slammed it shut.

"Arielle!" the voice called again.

Arielle turned around to see her best friend standing there. She moved to stand protectively in front of her locker and clutched her chest dramatically. "Oh God, Sarah, you scared me to death!"

"What are you still doing in here?" Sarah asked, looking at Arielle suspiciously. "The whole squad is waiting for you."

"Sorry," said Arielle, frowning as she examined her nails. "I chipped a nail during that gross frog experiment in biology class, and I just needed to fix it. I'm ready now. Let's go." It was a stupid lie, but the best she could come up with on such short notice. With luck, Sarah—and whoever else asked—would just accept it. She grabbed her water bottle and bag, and the two friends headed off to practice.

"B-T-W Arielle, I love the dress you had on today," Sarah said as they walked toward the gym. "You looked great, like always."

"I know, right," Arielle replied, without even thanking her for the compliment. She tossed her hair over her shoulder as she walked, feeling good about herself for having chosen today's cute outfit. It wasn't like that was *all* she cared about—but she knew how important it was to look good. So she went out of her way to do just that. Every day.

"And let's go shopping soon," said Sarah. "My cousin's Bat Mitzvah is next month, and I have to look good. You always know what looks best on me."

Arielle almost laughed. Sarah was beautiful and had great taste herself, so it was easy to choose outfits for her. She just didn't have enough confidence to pick them out *herself*.

"Sure, just say when. You know I'm always looking for an excuse to hit the mall." She hugged Sarah. "You'll be the most fashionable girl there. You just need to start having enough confidence to choose your outfits for yourself. You'll get there."

"Cool," answered Sarah with a smile. "Also, I've been meaning to ask. How on earth did you get an 'A' on our pop quiz in Bio? You *hate* doing biology experiments!"

Arielle's mouth twisted at the thought. "I don't enjoy cutting up slimy frogs, but I can memorize the process from books, no problem!" she said. "Totally different, dude."

"So," said Sarah, changing the subject, "do you think our squad is going to have the new routines ready by Friday? It's the biggest game of the year!"

"Duh, with me as your captain, how can you doubt it?" Arielle replied with another flip of her long blonde hair. "Come on, let's get to practice. Both schools will have huge crowds there on Friday, plus kids from other schools, and we have to be perfect!"

• • • •

After the girls warmed up, they practiced their latest routine. Arielle had always been good at twisting her body around. The school had wanted her to try out for the gymnastics team, but she'd chosen cheerleading instead. She loved nothing better than being at the center of all the action, cheering for the football and basketball teams, and amazing everyone with her fantastic tricks. Besides, it gave her something to do after school.

It also gave her a chance to hang out with all the coolest guys.

Halfway through practice, Ms. Brandt, the coach, signaled a short break. Arielle and Sarah, exhausted by the pace, shuffled over to their bags to get a drink. Arielle grabbed her cell phone and opened the camera—if there was anything she loved more than cheerleading, it was selfies.

She pushed her face close to Sarah's and grinning broadly said, "Say cheese!" She clicked the button and pulled the phone closer to look at the picture. "Not quite right," she said, glancing over at her friend again. "Quick, just one more. Smile!" she demanded as she caught a glimpse of Sarah's annoyed face.

"Hurry up, Arielle, there's no time now for selfies," Sarah complained. "Besides, I'm totally gross right now. All sweaty."

"There is *always* time for a quick selfie!" Arielle said with a wink.

Sarah smiled for the picture, then sighed. "Seriously, Arielle, this obsession with selfies is getting old. Everywhere we go, you have to post it on Instagram. Even if we're just hanging out doing homework, it's selfie this and post that. Don't you get sick of it? And don't even get me started on saying 'hashtag' *out loud* all the time."

Before Arielle could tell Sarah exactly why selfies were so important, Ms. Brandt clapped her hands and interrupted them. "All right girls," she said. "I'm happy with what I have seen today, so let's finish today's practice with the showstopper routine. Everyone, get into position."

As the girls began to take their positions, Ms. Brandt looked over at Arielle and Sarah and shrieked, "Arielle! Sarah! What on earth are you doing with your cell phones? Get over here, right now!"

"#WhyToScream!" muttered Arielle. She dropped her cell phone in her bag, and the girls hurried over to the rest of the team. "What's up with her? She obviously doesn't know I have finally cracked the one-thousand-follower mark on Instagram."

Sarah giggled and tugged on her friend's arm. "I totally agree, but we'd better hurry up before Ms. Brandt flips out!"

The cheerleaders lined up in the center of the gym. The music began, and they started their routine. Arielle stood on the sidelines, anxiously awaiting her big moment. As the music began to change, Ms. Brandt signaled to Arielle. She took a deep breath and dashed across the gym floor. She launched herself off the ground, gained momentum by bouncing off a teammate's shoulders, and twisted herself into a double-corkscrew. She tucked herself into the final tumble and landed gracefully, both feet firmly planted on the floor.

The girls clapped and cheered as Arielle executed an animated curtsy and smoothed down her ruffled hair. She was good, and she knew it.

"You are going to be the talk of the school again!" Sarah said as she high-fived her friend.

"I know, right," Arielle grinned. "#NumberOne! Let's try it again!"

"Okay," Sarah agreed. "Just give me a few minutes to call my mom and let her know I'm going to be home a bit late. She gets totally panicked when I'm not home right after practice."

Ms. Brandt congratulated the squad on how they had mastered the routine and dismissed them for the day.

• • • •

With practice over, the gym cleared out in a matter of minutes, and soon only Arielle and Sarah remained. Arielle saw that Sarah was still on the phone with her mom and groaned.

Suddenly she decided to push herself to the limit. She already knew she could handle it. Arielle was blessed with plenty of confidence in herself and her abilities. This was the perfect chance to practice her moves some more. Since the rest of the team had already left, she needed something to bounce off to get enough height and momentum. As she glanced around the gym, looking for something suitable, she spotted the balance beam the gymnastics team used.

*That'll do just fine*, she thought as she prepared to run over to it. *If I start from here, I'll gain enough speed to really fly through the air.*

She started running, moving faster and faster until she took a huge leap and threw herself toward the balance beam. With her hands landing squarely where they were supposed to, she flipped her legs elegantly upward into a complicated move that would have her twisting and turning for what seemed like ages in the air. But as she launched herself upward, she felt a strong gust of wind beneath her.

*That's weird*, she thought. *We're inside.*

She didn't think too much more about the wind—she had to concentrate on getting her moves right—but this time felt strangely different. Usually when she performed her stunts, she could feel herself going up and then coming back down again as she worked her way through the routine. But now, she felt as though she was suspended in the air … and when she looked down, she got the fright of her life!

Beneath her was what looked like a mini-cyclone, and it seemed to be propping her up. She was flying? No, that couldn't be right … could it?

She looked over at Sarah to see if she had seen what was happening, but she was still chatting with her mom, looking out the gym window and twirling her hair around her fingers. She had her back to Arielle, and besides, Arielle knew her friend could only pay attention to one thing at a time.

Time seemed to stand still, and Arielle felt as though she was up in the air for ages. Suddenly her stomach lurched with that awful feeling that lets you know you're falling.

# Fifteen Years Later

Almost instantly, she hit the ground with a loud *thud*. She let out a scream, and that finally got Sarah's attention. She quickly ended the call and rushed over to her friend, who was lying in a crumpled, ungraceful heap on the gym floor.

"Arielle, are you okay?" Sarah began. "What happened? Are you hurt? Oh my God, do we need to call an ambulance?" She'd gone into what Arielle called rambling mode, totally absorbed in the drama of the moment.

*Humph*, thought Arielle, *she really is all about the drama.* And she would have said something smart—like she usually did—but the truth was, she was confused and scared. Something extraordinary had just happened. She could swear she had seen a cyclone beneath her, making her fly. But the more she thought about it, the crazier it seemed. *I must be worn out and dizzy from all those twists and turns,* she told herself.

"I'm all right," she said as she took Sarah's hand and pulled herself up.

"Then what on earth just happened? I thought you had these moves totally down," exclaimed Sarah.

"Nothing happened," Arielle replied. "I just went too fast and made the wrong move, that's all. I'm fine now. Let's go."

The last thing she wanted to do was tell Sarah what had really happened. She wasn't even sure she believed it herself—and she knew Sarah would tell everyone else. Then, Arielle would not only have her own crazy mind to deal with—she'd also have to listen to the rest of the school asking questions and doubting her.

Not happening.

"And B-T-W," Arielle said with a flick of her long blonde hair, "can we please not mention this to anyone?"

Sarah nodded.

"In fact," Arielle continued, "let's just forget it ever happened!"

# Tara

"So hot and dry again today," Tara said to herself as she snuck out of the house. "When are we going to get some rain around here?"

The weather had certainly been strange lately—though she didn't know if she understood exactly why that was. Still, understanding or not, it was a fact of life. California was in trouble, and she doubted that they could expect rain anytime soon. *I'd better make sure I water my special flower every day before school, or it's sure to dry up and die in this hot "winter" weather we're having,* she thought.

She'd brought the watering can out, to do just that. She carefully balanced it as she walked, trying desperately not to spill any. *Every drop matters*, she thought over and over to herself.

She still wasn't sure why she wanted to keep her "special flower" a secret, but something in her gut told her she should…at least for now. She walked past the big oak tree she liked to climb and headed to the farthest corner of the garden, far away from any prying eyes in the house. As her plant came into view, Tara smiled to herself. The plant never failed to amaze her, not only with its beauty, but also its uniqueness. It grew straight up like a flower stem, and had lots of vines twisting around it. At the top, a bright green bulb was starting to form. She could hardly wait to see the beautiful exotic flower she felt certain would burst out one day.

*I'll tell my folks when it blooms*, she promised herself. That way it wouldn't seem so much like a deliberate secret, but more of a surprise. As the water flowed through the spout of the watering can into the earth surrounding the plant, she thought back to the day she found the seed.

She had been with her family on another one of their travel adventures. Tara loved to travel around the world, exploring the nature and cultures of different countries and, of course, meeting different animals. Everything on earth had a reason for being there, she'd always thought, and she never tired of seeing a sunset or discovering a new type of tree.

Tara had been exploring the Redwood Forest in Northern California when she wandered off the trail, following a black-tailed deer that seemed to communicate to her with his eyes. The deer soon started behaving strangely, digging its front hooves into a patch of mossy earth. The deer seemed agitated, so Tara observed him from afar and remained hidden behind a bush. She knew it sounded silly, but the deer had appeared to be irritated with her *because* she was hiding. However, Tara had enough respect for wild animals to make sure she kept a good distance from them. After a few minutes, when the deer seemed to realize she wouldn't come any closer, it let out a loud "huff" through its nostrils, turned, and bolted off into the bushes.

When she was sure the coast was clear, Tara crept out from behind the bush and went over to the mound of moss where the deer had been digging. There she saw a groove where the deer had dug through, and nestled inside was a large seed of the most brilliant emerald green Tara had ever seen. It was so bright it almost seemed to glow. She reached out and touched the seed with the tip of her index finger, then quickly drew it back in shock.

When she touched it, very thin, light-green veins started to spread out all over the seed. They looked like alien veins!

She looked all around her, but saw she was still alone—no one was watching, or playing a trick on her. So she took a deep, calming breath and bravely reached out for the seed again. She picked it up and held it in her palm, marveling at how cool it felt against her sweaty skin. There was something odd about the seed, though—almost as if it was buzzing in her hand. Almost as if it held a special kind of magic inside.

But that was silly, she told herself. Seeds couldn't possibly be magical. Still, despite her reasoning, she had felt drawn to it in a way she couldn't explain. She closed her fingers around it and rushed back to join her parents on their hike. When they got back to the campsite, Tara tucked the seed out of sight—for reasons she didn't quite understand—in a small compartment of her backpack, and tried to enjoy the rest of her holiday.

But she just could not get the seed out of her head.

As soon as she arrived back home, tired after the long drive, she rushed out to the far corner of the backyard to plant her secret seed. Her parents didn't think this was strange behavior. Tara often spent time meditating in the yard or climbing the big old oak tree, so she knew she was unlikely to be disturbed. She chose what she thought was the perfect spot, planted and watered the seed, and prepared herself for a long wait to watch it grow.

She was shocked, therefore, when returning to water the seed three days later, she found a plant shooting straight out of the ground, already knee-high!

She had been tending her plant for nearly two weeks now, and still had not told a soul. It kept growing, though, and she could see that it was close to blooming. Tara emptied the last of the water, wondering again what the flower would look like, and headed back to the house to get ready for school.

Today was a big day—she hoped to recruit volunteers to help her clean up the beach on Friday after school. Tara liked to do it at least once a month. She loved the beauty of the beach and liked keeping it clean, not only for people to enjoy but also for the animals living there. Litter could be dangerous for animals because it often looked like food. But when they tried to eat it, they could choke and even die.

Accordingly, Tara always looked for plastic bags, straws, and sharp things like disposable knives and forks. She hoped people would join her and be excited about the opportunity to help.

Her last attempt at getting people to volunteer, at the animal shelter, had not gone well. She'd ended up bathing and walking a dozen dogs that day, all on her own. She was determined that today would be better.

● ● ● ●

By the end of the school day, Tara had to admit that things were *not* better. She tugged at her pigtails irritably, causing the flower tucked behind her ear to fall onto the table. She picked it up and tucked it back behind her ear while she looked down at the list in front of her. *Two names*, she thought. *Two measly names! And they only volunteered to help me clean up the beach because they're new members of the biology club, and I'm the president.*

She sighed again as she started pulling down her conservation posters and packing up her things. Not even the free bookmarks she was offering had helped. And though her table was right in front of the school, people passed by her all day without even a glance.

"Oh well," she mumbled. "I'll take what I can get. Two is better than none, I guess."

As she stashed her things in her locker and made her way back outside, a voice shouted her name.

"Hey, Tara!"

She turned, wondering who could still be in the hallways. She grinned. It was Evan, one of the two boys who had signed up.

"Oh, hello Evan," she said, waiting for him. "How are you?"

He caught up to her, glancing nervously up and down the hallway as if he had something important to say, and didn't want to be overheard. "Umm, Tara, I know Jim and I promised to help you clean up the beach on Friday, but umm, you see, we just remembered that the game between the two biggest rival schools in Santa Monica is the same day and, well, we really want to get there early and check out the cheerleaders. We heard that one of the schools has one who looks like she flies…and, well, that's way cooler than picking up trash on the beach. We'll help you some other time, okay?"

He turned on his heel and ran back down the corridor and out of sight before Tara could get a single word out.

She absolutely could not believe what she'd just heard. "Flying cheerleaders," she muttered crossly. "That can't be for real. And how on earth does he think that's more important than…well, the earth?"

She headed for home in a gloomy mood. *Oh well*, she thought. *It won't be the first time I'm picking up trash at the beach on my own. It would be nice to have some company, but at least I know I'm making a difference to the planet, not wasting my time watching silly cheerleaders!* She rarely got angry, but now she felt like kicking something. She hated feeling like that. She needed to do something to restore her harmony and balance.

Luckily, she knew exactly what to do. She picked up the pace, eager to get home and see her best friends. Tara wasn't like other girls her age, who hung out with a gaggle of girlfriends. No, her best friends were a pet ferret, a chinchilla, four dogs, and what she believed was the world's laziest cat. Remus spent all day sleeping in a sunbeam and at night curled up at the foot of Tara's bed, purring softly. The only time he was energetic was when he was hungry!

Tara's pets were not just pets, though—they were family, and each had come into her life by what she believed was fate. In fact, she had rescued all of them. First, she adopted Remus from the shelter when she heard he would be put down if nobody gave him a home. Then her neighbors had called animal control to get rid of the ferret that kept sneaking into their homes to look for food. Tara had caught and hidden it when she saw the truck coming, named him Freddy, and slowly tamed him. He was now better behaved than her dogs!

Each of the four dogs had been strays when she found them. Tara knew that they would have surely ended up in the pound, but she had started feeding them, and naturally they ended up following her home and simply refused to leave. Chester the chinchilla had actually belonged to a classmate. His mother decided the rodent was a nuisance and had to go when she found him gnawing on her favorite pair of shoes. Tara offered to take him in.

Fortunately, Tara's parents were also animal lovers. But she knew she had pushed her luck as far as she dared —"no more strays," they told her.

Still, her pets gave her love and loyalty, and right now, she needed that more than anything else. She rounded the final corner to her house and picked up speed. It was time to take the dogs for their walk, and she knew how much they hated it when she was late. She entered her yard to a chorus of barks and licks and quickly dashed inside to drop off her bag and get their leashes. She gave Freddy a quick cuddle and scratched Remus behind his ears. He just stretched lazily in response, not even bothering to open his eyes. She ran back outside, put the leashes on the dogs, and hurried out the gate with them.

As usual, she enjoyed being outside and began whistling happily.

Passers-by gave her funny looks as she told her dogs about the frustrations of her day. She ignored them and kept up a happy stream of chatter. What she did notice, though, was Lance and Rudy Prodigus walking with their father, Max, on the opposite side of the street. Everyone in Santa Monica knew the Prodigus family. They were

super-rich because Mr. Prodigus owned many of the businesses in town, and always seemed to be building more. They lived on a fancy estate and drove big cars.

Tara watched the Prodigus clan as they unwrapped their ice cream treats. What they did next made her jaw drop open. They tossed the wrappers onto the sidewalk!

She couldn't believe what she'd seen. So she waited until it was safe to cross the street and hurried over toward where they were standing.

"Mr. Prodigus!" she called. "Mr. Prodigus!"

Fifteen Years Later

He stopped and looked at her with a puzzled expression. "Umm, do I know you? How can I help you?" he asked. "That's a lot of dogs you're trying to walk."

"Yes, sir," she replied as politely as she could. "I do need some help, actually. I need you to please pick up those ice cream wrappers you just threw on the ground. That's littering, you know, and it's super-bad for the environment. There's a trash can right over there." She pointed to a big trash bin on the corner.

"I beg your pardon!" he shouted. "How rude! I'm not sure who you think you are, telling me what to do. You're just a little girl!"

"Sir, I realize I'm just a girl, but I'm also just asking you to respect our earth and our town. If we all do our part, the earth can stay healthy and beautiful for us all to enjoy. There's no reason for you to just throw your trash on the ground like it doesn't matter."

The man huffed indignantly again. "Come on, boys. Let's go home."

Tara sighed. Why was it always the same response? It wasn't that hard to throw something away, surely, and being rich didn't mean that they didn't have to take care of the planet — or follow the laws. She picked up the ice cream wrappers and tossed them into the bin herself. She was starting to feel really down, though. First the boys who didn't want to help clean the beach, and now this. Didn't people understand the importance of keeping their world clean?

As evening approached, she headed home with the dogs, now tired from their walk. When she got home, she did what she usually did when she felt upset or stressed: climb the enormous old oak tree in her back yard. She swung herself up to her favorite branch and sat resting her chin in her hands, feeling defeated and frustrated. She didn't know why, but being so high up and completely surrounded by the tree helped calm her spirit. She leaned back against the thick trunk, closed her eyes, and started feeling the tension drain from her body. As she relaxed, she heard a little squeaking sound and smiled. The squirrels had come to say hello. It seemed strange for wild creatures to be so comfortable around her and allow her to get so close. But every time she climbed the tree, they came out to greet her.

"Hey, guys," she said. "I hope you've had a better day than me."

They squeaked and chattered back to her in response.

"Sometimes it feels like you guys actually understand what I'm saying," she said with a grin. She shook her head at how silly that sounded. People already thought she was nuts with the way she talked to animals. What would they think if they found out she thought they could talk *back*?

"You know what I saw today?" she asked. "A father teaching his sons to litter. They had ice cream treats and just threw the wrappers down on the ground without a thought. I *hate* it when people litter! There is no need for that. Even worse, there was a trash can right at the corner. Littering is super-bad for us, the animals, and the environment. I just don't understand why people do it." As dusk turned to night, she looked up at the beautiful and bright full moon surrounded by millions of sparkly stars, and said to herself, "I wish I had the power to make it right and help the earth somehow by changing the way people behave."

TARA'S SONG
**I WISH I HAD THE POWER**

*PLAY* this song at
TheSuperSustainables.com

Facing the Drought

She looked back at the squirrels. One had his head tilted to one side, as if he was really listening to her. She chuckled to herself again.

"Well, guys," she said, "thanks again for listening. I always feel so much better after chatting to you up here. See you soon."

This time, though, instead of hearing squirrely squeaks in return, Tara was sure she heard one squirrel say, "No problem, Tara, we're always here for you."

She nearly fell out of the tree, but grabbed a branch to steady herself, turned back to the squirrels, and said, "W-w-what did you say?"

The squirrels just squeaked back at her like they always had, before turning around and scurrying away.

"I must be going crazy," she said to herself. But try as she might, she couldn't get her hammering heart to slow down in her chest.

"Time to go meditate this all away," she decided.

And with shaking hands, she began to climb back down the tree.

# Franco

Franco's mom called it "his little thing with fire," and said it started when he was a baby. From a very young age, he seemed drawn to flames of all kinds, and stared at them for hours on end. When he was a toddler throwing tantrums, lighting a candle and letting him look at the flame tended to quiet even the wildest of rages.

His mom thought it was cute and endearing until he was three and set fire to the living room curtains. She screamed at him, half in frustration, half in relief he hadn't been hurt. Nevertheless, she punished him, hoping he would learn his lesson and never do something so foolish and dangerous again.

Not long afterward, Franco began to show a keen interest in drawing and painting. One day when he was four, his parents had gone to work as usual and left him with Cindy, his babysitter. About noon, Cindy gave him some coloring books and crayons to keep him busy while she prepared lunch. It seemed to work well, as Franco stayed quietly in his room coloring.

But after half an hour had passed and lunch was ready, Cindy started to think he had been unusually quiet for such a hyperactive kid.

"Franco!" she called. "Lunch is ready!" When Franco didn't respond she panicked, thinking something had happened to him. She raced up the stairs two at a time and flung open his bedroom door. Her mouth fell open in shock at what she saw.

There was Franco, calmly drawing all over the walls in his room.

"Franco!" she shrieked. "What do you think you're doing?"

Franco turned to face her with the most angelic smile on his face. He was clutching his three favorite colors — orange, red, and yellow — and if she hadn't been so angry, she would have been seriously impressed by his talent. He had drawn flames all over the walls, and the way he had blended the colors to create a flame effect was amazing. Cindy could tell he had a future ahead of him as a talented artist, but knew that it would be a challenge to get him to display this talent in the right way.

His mom knew the only punishment that would have any real effect was confiscating his art supplies. She gave them back a week later and he'd kept right on drawing. Over the years, his drawings had become very intricate, detailed, and advanced for his age. Giving him some paper and crayons or paint ensured that he was occupied for hours, creating amazing works of art.

At least, she'd thought, he'd stopped setting things on fire. His art might consume him, but it never did any damage she could see.

As Franco got older, he became a typical guy's guy, and was very popular at school. He liked hanging out with his buddies, and together they would go skateboarding at Venice Beach, to auto shows and races, or the park to play football. He had a select group of close friends, though many other kids wanted to be his friend. He was his school's star quarterback, and had automatic "cool kid" status because of that. However, what most people didn't know was that deep down, Franco was actually a really good guy with a big heart. Because he would never snitch on his buddies, he often took the blame when bad things happened.

Most recently, one of his best friends, Marco, had started a fight with some of the players from a rival team. Franco got pulled into it to protect his friend, and ended up taking the blame for starting it when the principal, Mr. Thomas, called him in to explain what happened.

Franco was smart enough to realize that most of his problems in life were a result of not thinking things through properly. Around town he was labeled a troublemaker, but he didn't think that was fair. The real issue, if he was very honest, was that he was too spontaneous — the type of kid who did things on the spur of the moment. His mom always scolded him in frustration and said things like, "You're a smart boy, so why don't you ever think before you act? I raised you better than this."

But he was impulsive by nature — that was just who he was. Someone who acted exactly the way he felt, when he felt it. And things always seemed to be a good idea...until they weren't. That part he couldn't deny was his fault, but what had always puzzled him was that if his ideas were so bad, why were others always so ready to go along with him?

Now that he was in high school, Franco had been told numerous times by Mr. Thomas that he had to watch how he behaved because he was a natural leader and other kids were bound to follow his example. But this didn't sit well with Franco. He had never set out to make himself a leader, and really didn't want the responsibility that came along with it. If people chose to follow him, well, that was their choice, he guessed. And if they got into trouble for it, they would have to man up and take their medicine — just like he did when he got caught misbehaving.

But he never got his friends in trouble. In fact, he took responsibility for things that he hadn't done, just to keep other people *out* of trouble! So where was the part about people having *his* back? When was everyone else going to start taking care of *him* the way he took care of them?

Franco tried not to spend too much time dwelling on his conduct. He often thought to himself that it was just who he was, that he just did what he had to do. It wasn't a completely satisfactory answer, but it was all he had. For the moment.

FRANCO'S SONG
**I AM WHAT I AM**

**PLAY** this song at
TheSuperSustainables.com

One lazy Sunday morning, Franco was still sleeping when the tapping sound of small stones hitting his window, one after another, woke him up. "Come ooooon!" he muttered, pulling the covers over his head to block out the sound.

*TAP, TAP, PLINK, PLINK.*

*What on earth is that noise?* he wondered to himself.

He turned over again and tried to go back to sleep, but at that moment, his window sounded like it was going to shatter. He threw the covers back in frustration, realizing that more sleep was not going to happen, rubbed his face wearily, then got up. Irritated, he walked over to the window to see what was so important, muttering the whole way, "Why can't you let me sleep? It's Sunday, for crying out loud! Can't whoever it is just go away until later?! For their sake, this had better be really important!"

He pulled his red curtains aside and a flood of bright sunlight nearly blinded him. Franco, still half asleep, struggled to open his eyes. *Ugh, I can't even open my eyes,* he thought, then absentmindedly added, *It sure is bright for the middle of winter.*

He rubbed his eyes and forced them open as he slid the window up. Two of his best friends, Marco and Armando, stood in his yard holding their skateboards.

"What are you guys doing here so early?" he asked.

"What do you mean early, dude?" Marco said. "It's almost noon. Did you forget that we planned to go to the auto show together? Today is the last day, and we don't want to miss it!"

"Oh, that's right!" Franco groaned. "I totally forgot, guys, sorry."

And he should have remembered. This show only came to town once every two years, and Franco hadn't missed one since the age of eight. He loved nothing more than to see the latest models and futuristic designs of the concept cars. He had to get there today— he especially wanted to see the new electric models and take more photos to add to his collection.

Besides, the show meant a lot to him. The very first time he'd gone, it had been with his dad. They'd spent the whole day taking photos of the cars and trying to pick a favorite. The following week, his dad had come home from work with a surprise for Franco—he'd printed out all the photos they had taken and bought him a special photo album. Franco remembered spending many happy hours arranging the photos and studying the car designs, and it was now a tradition that when the show came to town, he would photograph the cars and add them to his album.

That day, spending time with just his dad, doing "boy stuff," was one of his favorite childhood memories. Unfortunately, his dad had never taken him back to the show because he was always too busy with work. So Franco went with his two closest friends instead.

"Okay, hold on, *amigos*. I'll be down in ten minutes," he said. But when he stepped back from the window, he turned too quickly and bumped his head on the edge. "*Ouch!!!*"

And like all his other friends, these two just laughed at him.

"Hurry, but stay in one piece, dude," Armando said.

Franco pressed his lips together, wishing he could stop being cool, just once—just long enough to tell his friends it wasn't always funny when he got hurt or got in trouble. Just once, he wished people would act like they cared as much as he did.

But admitting that would lose him so many cool points that he knew he'd never do it.

Instead, he just waved at them and then dashed around his room, putting on his clothes and grabbing his hat and skateboard before running downstairs. The three of them hopped on their skateboards and raced each other all the way to the show.

● ● ● ●

When they left the show that afternoon, all Franco could talk about was the cars. "Did you see that hot red car with the doors that opened upward and the fire prints on them?" he asked for the tenth time. "So cool! Can't believe I almost missed it. I'm lucky to have you guys— thanks so much for waking me up."

"Sure," Marco responded with a smile.

"We couldn't have gone without you; it wouldn't be the same," Armando agreed with a nod.

The guys sat on a high wall near the street and talked about everything they'd seen. As they chatted, Franco lifted his arm to wave to Emanuel, his cousin, who was walking down the street, carrying a few cans of spray paint. "Hey, buddy!" he called out.

"Hey, guys," Emanuel responded.

"What are you doing with all the spray paint?" asked Franco.

"I 'borrowed' it from my sister, who's working on some art project for school. She's not home now, so I thought I'd take it. You know, decorate some of the walls around here," he answered with a grin.

"Oh, cool!" said Armando.

"Which wall are you planning to paint?" asked Marco.

"The wall under the bridge near the school. Nobody's around there at this time," Emanuel answered. "Do you guys want to join me? Franco, you're a great artist. Let's paint something really cool there."

Marco and Armando both agreed, practically jumping with excitement, but Franco shook his head resolutely. The last time he'd let Emanuel talk him into something like this, he'd found himself in deep trouble. Mostly because Emanuel's ideas tended to be against the law.

"No, Emanuel, the last thing I need right now is to get in more trouble. Mr. Thomas will kill me if I end up in his office again," he said firmly.

"Come on, Franco, no one will know you were involved. We'll do it together, so if one of us gets caught, we'll all get caught. All for one!" Emanuel said, trying to pressure Franco.

"Yeah, let's do it, Franco," said Marco. "He's right. You're the best artist in school, and you'll do a way better job than us three."

"Yeah, come on," echoed Armando.

Franco knew they were wrong—it wouldn't be all for one if they got caught, and people would be bound to know it was him because everyone knew his artwork. So the moment anyone saw it, they'd realize who had done it.

Still, the three stared at him so expectantly that he felt awful for saying no the first time. "Okay, okay, guys. But you're sure that nobody is around, right?" he asked Emanuel.

"I'm sure," responded Emanuel. "I walked by there earlier and the place was totally deserted. I promise. No one's going to see us!"

Franco turned his hat around on his head—a sign that he was in and ready to go— and said, "Okay, let's go. But remember whose idea this was!"

"Yeah!" they all said in unison. Marco and Armando took some of the spray paint from Emanuel, then grabbed their skateboards and walked toward the bridge. Franco went along, trying to put his doubts aside. They weren't going to get caught, anyhow, and if they did he would just count on Emanuel to come clean. This had been his idea—surely he'd admit to that.

When they arrived at the wall, Franco took another look around to make sure no one else was there. "Okay, it seems safe," he said confidently.

Armando, Marco, and Emanuel set the spray paint down and

propped their skateboards up against the wall. Franco was still feeling so inspired by the car show that all he could see in his mind was that bright red car with the flames on the doors. "I know what I want to do," he said, suddenly excited.

The other guys laughed and nodded, then divided the wall into four sections—one for each of them. Franco took his hat off, put it down on a rock, and got started. He chose the largest section of the wall. Since they all knew his art would be the most beautiful, no one argued with him over having the most space.

Facing the Drought

After armour, Marco, Armando, and Emanuel finished their sections, while Franco continued to work. The other three sat near Franco to watch him work, trying not to bother him.

"Wow!" said Armando, "that's amazing!"

"Looks like the car we saw at the show," Marco added as they all admired Franco's latest creation.

FUEGO!

Fifteen Years Later

While Marco and Armando stayed with Franco to keep him company, Emanuel decided to make sure they were still alone. He climbed up the grass bank they had descended to get under the bridge and looked around. He didn't see anyone, which made him happy. But as he was heading back to rejoin the others, a bright flash of light struck his eyes. *Oh wow, what's that?* he asked himself. He went over to look and discovered a piece of a broken magnifying glass, reflecting the sun. He bent down to pick it up and another idea popped into his head.

A smile spread across his face as he remembered seeing a movie that showed how to start a fire from the sun with just a magnifying glass and dry grass.

*I guess it's a good time to see if it really works,* he thought.

He looked around at the grass and thought, *It hasn't rained here in a long time. This grass should be good and dry and easy to burn.* He picked some dry grass and placed it in a small pile. Then he arranged a few small rocks to hold the magnifying glass in place. He angled it toward the sun and pushed the dry grass directly underneath.

After a few minutes, nothing had happened. He frowned, frustrated.

"I guess it was just a stupid movie. I knew it wouldn't work," he muttered.

Then he heard the other guys calling his name. He left the magnifying glass where it was and ran back to the bridge.

"Where have you been?" asked Franco, suspicious. He knew his cousin, and knew Emanuel got in more trouble than anyone else. He'd been gone for a lot longer than it would take to make sure no one else was around.

"I just wanted to make sure no one was coming," answered Emanuel. "Oh wow, Franco. You finished it. This is so cool. Everyone's going to love it!"

Franco smiled. "It did turn out pretty good, didn't it?" he asked, forgetting Emanuel's explanation. "Now let's get out of here before someone shows up."

The boys started gathering up the spray paint when suddenly they noticed smoke blowing under the bridge.

●　●　●　○

"Where's this smoke coming from?" asked Marco, confused.

Emanuel paused, and a look came over his face that Franco recognized.

"Emanuel, what did you do?" he asked.

"Nothing!" Emanuel said quickly. "It's probably nothing."

But Franco could smell the smoke, and was sure he saw an orange glow coming from the grassy area.

He'd know that glow anywhere—it was fire. And with how dry the area was, it would take no time to spread. "There's a fire!" he shouted. "We have to get out of here!"

They quickly grabbed everything and ran out from under the bridge.

Franco realized that he'd forgotten his hat. "I have to go back for my hat!" he shouted, panicked.

"No!" said Marco. "You can't go back under there. It's too dangerous now."

Marco was right—someone had already called the fire department, and the boys could hear the sirens in the distance. If they got caught at the scene, they were going to be in big trouble.

"Dude, we have to leave *now*, before it's too late," said Armando.

"Yes, now!" agreed Emanuel.

Franco looked under the bridge and saw that the smoke had become thicker. There was no way he could go back for his hat. "Okay, guys, let's separate and meet up tomorrow to talk about this," he said.

They ran off in different directions.

● ● ● ●

The next day, Franco, Marco, Armando, and Emanuel met up at school to talk about what had happened at the bridge.

Franco began. "Okay, guys, does anyone know how the fire started? We need to clear things up now before someone traces it back to us."

"I have no idea," said Marco.

"Me neither," said Armando, shrugging his shoulders. "I just smelled the smoke when we started picking up all our stuff."

Emanuel sat quietly with his head down. "Emanuel, do you know something about the fire?" Franco asked. "You're the only one who went out from under the bridge. Did you see anything? Did you *do* something?"

Emanuel met his cousin's gaze and his eyes filled with tears. "Yes, I did it," he admitted. "It's all my fault." As tears ran down his cheeks, Emanuel confessed the whole story to his friends. "I'm so sorry, guys."

He looked thoroughly ashamed of himself and terrified at what their reaction was going to be.

Marco stood up, and shouted, "Why didn't you say something

yesterday? Why did you let us believe that somehow it was *our* fault? If we get in trouble because of this, it's going to be *your* fault. This was *all* your idea!"

"He's right," added Armando. "I can't get in trouble for this now. My father will kill me. Besides, it was your fault. We didn't have anything to do with the fire!"

Marco and Armando were livid and continued shouting at Emanuel, but Franco held his hand up.

"Okay, guys, cool down."

But they continued, and now they were starting to draw the looks of other kids. If they weren't careful, they were going to arouse suspicion just by fighting.

Franco stood up and raised his voice. "Okay! That's enough! What's done is done. There's no use screaming and shouting about it now."

Marco and Armando stopped shouting, but Emanuel was still crying. They all looked at Franco's angry face. "But Franco —" began Marco.

"No buts," responded Franco. "Turning on Emanuel is not going to help anything. We are all in this together, and we will deal with this like men." He sat back down, looked at the fear in their faces, and in that second made up his mind about what he was going to do.

"You guys can relax. You're going to be fine," he told them

● ● ● ●

The next day, Franco chewed vigorously on a piece of gum and fiddled with the hem of his shirt as he waited outside the principal's office. It would be nothing short of a miracle if he *wasn't* suspended.

The secretary's phone rang suddenly, interrupting his thoughts, and Franco saw her glance up at him with a stern face. It was time.

"Mr. Thomas will see you now, Franco. Put your skateboard over here, out of the way, and go into his office and close the door behind you," the secretary told him.

"Yes, ma'am," he replied, standing up and smoothing down his shirt.

"Franco," she said. He turned to face her, still chewing on his gum. "Spit out the gum," she warned. "You're in enough trouble already!"

Franco spat his gum into the trash bin. Despite all the trouble he seemed to find himself in, it was always a bit daunting coming into the principal's office, especially when you knew you were done for.

"Sit down, Franco," Mr. Thomas said, gesturing to the chairs on the opposite side of his big oak desk.

Franco perched himself on the edge of the chair and met the principal's eyes for the first time since entering the office. Mr. Thomas flung a hat on the desk and asked, "Did you forget something under the bridge?"

Franco was startled. He had forgotten all about his hat!

Mr. Thomas continued, "This was given to me by one of the police officers, who found it under the bridge, next to the graffiti on the wall and close to where the fire started. And I happen to remember seeing this hat before." Mr. Thomas looked straight into Franco's eyes, waiting for a response, but Franco just stared at the hat, speechless.

This had *not* been part of his plan.

"All right, Franco," Mr. Thomas began, breaking the painful silence. "You don't have to say anything. After all, it's pretty easy to tell that you played a role in all this—the graffiti, the fire, and this hat. Everything you like most. Care to explain yourself?"

"Well, s-s-s-sir," Franco stammered, "it's not what you're thinking,

Mr. Thomas."

"Not what I'm thinking?" boomed Mr. Thomas. "Do you have any *idea* of the damage you caused, and how much pressure you have put me under? I'm tempted to pull you off the football team as punishment!"

Franco's eyes widened in disbelief. He'd considered the possibility of being suspended from school, but never imagined he could lose his place on the team. Especially this week—it was the week of the big game, and he was the school's best quarterback, despite being a year or two younger than his teammates!

Mr. Thomas paused for effect. Before he could continue, there was a knock at the door, and the secretary opened it. "I'm sorry to interrupt, sir, but a parent out here insists on speaking with you right away."

"This is really not a good time, Meyera," Mr. Thomas said with a sigh.

"I know, sir," Meyera began. "I tried to tell her."

"Okay, let's get on with it, then," Mr. Thomas said. "Franco, wait here, I'll be right back."

Mr. Thomas left Franco hanging, thinking the worst about the outcome he faced. He was so nervous that he just could not stop fidgeting. *How could I have been so dumb as to get into trouble the week of the big game? ARRGH!* he thought. *If I don't play, our team is doomed.*

He was so engrossed in his negative thoughts that he didn't notice what was happening with his fingers until it was too late. He jumped up in absolute shock as he realized his jeans were on fire, and started slapping his pants to put out the flames. Miraculously, he was unharmed, as had always been the case when he encountered fire.

But that didn't answer the question about how the fire had started.

At that very moment, Mr. Thomas walked back into the office! "What are you doing!?" he shouted.

Franco looked up in shock. "Umm, nothing, sir," he stammered. "There was a spider crawling up my leg."

"Well, sit down now so we can continue our discussion," Mr. Thomas said as he took his seat opposite Franco. Fortunately, he didn't seem to notice the burn holes in Franco's jeans.

Franco sat down, but he barely heard a word Mr. Thomas said. Was he going crazy? Had he really just seen flames appear from his fingertips? He looked down at the holes with the scorch marks around the edges. He glanced at his hands, wondering, but couldn't figure it out.

How had that fire started?

*Ay Dios Mio*, he thought. *This just can't be real.*

Mr. Thomas shouted his name and snapped him out of his scared and confused thoughts.

"*Franco!* You need to answer me!" Mr. Thomas said loudly in his no-nonsense-and-don't-mess-with-me voice. "What on earth were you thinking? That bridge is on school property. Why the graffiti, and lighting a fire on top of it?"

"I really didn't mean to cause any harm, sir," Franco said. "And about the graffiti, you're right. I'll take responsibility for that. But the fire was a mistake. I didn't mean to cause a fire."

"Mistake?" asked Mr. Thomas. "How can you set a fire by *mistake*?"

At that point, Franco tried to remember Emanuel's story about how it happened. "So, what happened was…" He began telling Emanuel's story, but changed it to sound like he had caused it instead. After all, he was already in trouble—was there any point in getting Emanuel in trouble too?

"I cannot believe you did that!" responded Mr. Thomas. "All because of a silly movie you watched? Did you really have to try it to know that it works? Haven't you noticed that everything is so dry around here? Fires can start far too easily.

"That's your problem all over again, Franco. You never think things through properly, and these kinds of impulsive actions always land you in hot water. I have spoken to your teachers. They all say you are really smart, but you just don't apply yourself. Some of them think the only way to give you the wake-up call you need is to ban you from playing football. Is that what it's going to take for you to get serious about your schoolwork?"

Franco hung his head. "Please, sir, don't pull me from the team. I'll do whatever I have to do to make it right. I'll even go to detention every single day and study really hard, but please let me play."

"I'm really not sure," said Mr. Thomas. "I need to think about it. I also know that you couldn't possibly have pulled this off by yourself. And knowing you, I'm sure you were surrounded by some accomplices. I want to know who else was involved. Give me their names, Franco. *Now!*"

"It was just me, really!" Franco insisted. He was in trouble, and he would go down for it by himself, regardless of the consequences. No need for anyone else to get involved.

Unless they gave themselves up. But Franco knew they wouldn't. As usual, they'd all be completely satisfied to let Franco take the fall for them. They probably wouldn't even say thank you.

"I'm the stupid one who caused the fire." He hung his head, feeling ashamed and wondering if he was just that—stupid. Why was it that he always got caught? Why didn't anyone else get in trouble?

Even worse—was he naive for always taking the blame? Should he stand up for himself, just once?

He wasn't surprised when Mr. Thomas didn't buy it. "You have to stop being so impulsive and start thinking about the consequences of what you do, before you do it," he said.

"You're right sir, and I really am sorry."

Mr. Thomas sighed and ran his hands through his hair. "I don't think you actually are, Franco. I think you're sorry you got caught, not sorry for what you did. And I don't think you have any intention of learning from your mistake, and figuring out that your friends aren't going to protect you the way you protect them. Luckily for you, your coach has made it clear that without you on the team, our school doesn't have much chance of winning the game on Friday, so you can play—"

Franco quickly raised his head with a big smile. "Oh, thank you, sir, thank you so much! I promise to throw lots of touchdown passes, so you'll be proud of me."

"Don't get ahead of yourself, Franco. You can play, but there are going to be some serious consequences for what you did yesterday. Did you really think that putting graffiti on school property and starting a fire would go unpunished?"

Franco realized that any response at this point would likely just dig a deeper hole for him, so he remained silent. Besides, it wasn't like he didn't know. He knew exactly what he'd done wrong—and that most of it hadn't been his fault. Mr. Thomas couldn't tell him anything to make him feel worse than he already did.

"Also, I am going to call your parents in for a meeting about this. Hopefully they will be able to convince you to tell me who else was involved. And I'm also going to ask them to monitor what movies you watch a lot more closely in the future. You may go back to class now."

"Yes, sir," Franco said, and stood up. But he wasn't that worried about it—he knew his parents would never make a meeting like that. And if they didn't meet, Mr. Thomas would have a harder time convincing Franco to tell him the names of his accomplices.

# Mizu

*I must be the only kid in Santa Monica not at the big football game today,* Mizu thought as he sat in the sand next to his surfboard at Santa Monica State Beach. But the truth was, he was far too shy to handle being in a noisy crowd. Plus he had never really understood the point of the sport. Mizu much preferred being in his room investigating new science stuff on his iPad or playing games on his iMac and using strategy to outsmart his competitors. He was kind of an "iSmart" kid.

Mizu prided himself on being a straight-A student. He was not only the president of the science club, but had also just competed in the All-State Science Olympiad. His project on tidal energy generators had earned him first prize out of fifty other projects.

Instead of making him popular, though, Mizu's academic ability seemed to have the opposite effect. Mizu knew the other kids at school thought he was a little weird and not cool enough to hang around. Sometimes feeling different all the time really bothered him … but he knew that being sensitive about it would only make things worse. Instead, he was careful to keep his true feelings a secret—which wasn't really all that hard, because he didn't have many friends. He had long ago stopped dwelling on the fact that if people took the time to get to know him a little, they would realize there was far more to him than just a science geek. These days, he just lived his life alone. And he was used to it. Kind of.

He sat staring out at the flat horizon, almost willing a big wave to appear so he could surf. Surfing was the only thing that calmed him down, especially after what had happened at school today. More than anything else, Mizu *loved* being in the water — which was why he headed to the beach whenever he was upset.

Mizu's mom always referred to him as a "water baby," and loved telling people the story of how he had learned to swim before he could walk. Apparently they had been visiting a friend when the 10-month-old Mizu crawled outside and dove into the pool. His mom said she had screamed and started crying, but just as she was about to dive in and rescue him, her friend grabbed her arm and pointed. She had nearly fainted when she saw Mizu paddling around the pool, laughing and giggling. From that day on his mom nicknamed him "Mizu"— Japanese for water.

After that, his love for water was so obvious that his parents seemed to forget that his real name was actually "Mitsue," which means "the light" in Japanese. They started introducing him to everyone as Mizu instead. He had never really minded this nickname because he always felt a close connection to the ocean waves, a feeling he couldn't explain.

The flat ocean was the "perfect" cherry on top of his bad day. He was thoroughly depressed and sad.

"I thought the winter waves would be bigger, but it feels more like summer. No wind, no waves," he mumbled to himself as he raked his fingers through his dark hair.

*It is the worst end to the worst day ever*, he thought to himself as he closed his eyes and recalled what happened just a few hours earlier.

Once again, he'd received a perfect score on his science quiz—which would have been great if Mr. Reichman had just handed him his paper like he did with everyone else. But no, Mr. Reichman had spent what felt like an eternity praising Mizu, not only for his great grade but also for all the extra work he had done, going above and beyond the original assignment by citing all the latest online research on the quiz. For his extra effort, Mr. Reichman had awarded him an extra ten percent over and above his 100 percent, making his final score a 110 percent. His teacher had meant well, trying to encourage the other students to go the extra mile, and on some level Mizu knew that. But he hated all the fuss. It made the other kids jealous, so they teased and mocked him.

For the rest of the day, as word spread about his grades, he endured sneers, teasing, and snide comments in the hallways. When he used the bathroom, one kid threw a soggy pile of toilet paper into his stall. It missed him by about an inch. He was proud of his grades, of course, because beyond being naturally intelligent, he *really* worked hard to get them. But he wished the teachers would stop making such an example of him. He already had trouble fitting in at school because he wasn't interested in the same sorts of things as the other kids. Pointing out that he was smarter than everyone else just made the differences more obvious.

And he'd found, over time, that kids didn't really like things that were different.

While Mizu was sitting and thinking about all this, the fire alarm sounded and the kids jumped up in a panic. Mr. Reichman told the kids to calm down and went out to the hall to see what was going on. It turned out to be just a drill because of what had recently happened at the public school across town, so he reassured his students that everything was fine and continued with the lesson.

After class ended, Mizu stayed back until all of the other kids left, as he usually did. Mr. Reichman looked at Mizu with pride and said, "Great job, Mizu, keep up the good work."

Little did Mr. Reichman realize how much trouble being the "smart kid" caused Mizu with the other kids.

Mizu looked back at Mr. Reichman as he was gathering his things to leave. He wanted to share his feelings, but couldn't get the words out. Instead he said weakly, "Sure, Mr. Reichman," and watched him leave the room.

Sitting all alone, Mizu sighed, and then got up to leave as well.

As he walked toward his locker to put his books away, Mizu pictured himself already at the beach getting ready to ride a big wave, which made him feel a bit better. He was so lost in his daydream that he bumped into Dylan, one of the coolest upperclassmen in school, and his tall, pretty blonde girlfriend Sandy. Mizu dropped his books and fell to the floor, while the cup of cold-pressed beet juice Sandy had been drinking spilled all over her white miniskirt.

Shocked and upset, she shouted at Mizu, "Oh my God! What's wrong with you, four-eyes?"

"I'm so sorry," stammered Mizu, kneeling on the floor gathering his books. "I didn't see you there." Embarrassed, he reached up and tried to help her clean her skirt.

"Take your hands off my girlfriend, dork!" shouted Dylan.

"Oh, I'm sorry. I didn't mean…" Mizu said, scared and confused as he let go of her skirt and stood up.

A bunch of other kids heard Dylan's raised voice from down the hall and gathered around the "hot spot" to see what was going on, creating a big circle around Dylan, Sandy, and Mizu.

"That's the nerd from my class," said one of the kids.

"Teach him a lesson, Dylan!" shouted one of Dylan's friends.

Breathing hard and terribly embarrassed, Mizu looked around for a way out of the situation. He still hadn't fully processed how he'd gotten himself into this mess, and how it was going downhill so quickly.

"Fight!" yelled one kid.

Others followed with "Fight!" Soon the entire circle was shouting, "Fight, fight, fight!"

Dylan loved the attention, and didn't want to disappoint them and ruin his reputation. He took off his jacket and handed it to Sandy.

"Are you ready, dork?" he asked Mizu, rolling up his sleeves. "The crowd wants a show."

Dylan was much bigger and stronger, and Mizu wasn't a fighter. Nor had he ever beaten anyone up or even thought about it. He glanced around at the crowd, which continued to grow in size and get louder. Dylan assumed a fighting stance and slapped Mizu in the face. "Are you ready, nerd? Let's do this! Come on, hit me back."

Mizu's glasses flew to the floor and the crowd cheered for Dylan to do it again. Mizu bent down to pick up his glasses, and Dylan got in position for the next punch. Mizu fearfully looked Dylan in the eyes, wishing this would all be over, and then out of the blue the fire alarm went off. The ceiling sprinklers started raining water over everyone in the hall.

Screaming, the kids panicked and quickly ran outside.

Within seconds, the hall was nearly empty. Only Dylan, Sandy, and Mizu remained. They were all soaking wet.

"Let's leave," said Sandy. "He's not worth it."

Dylan looked at Mizu once again and said, "You got lucky!" He took his jacket back from Sandy and they hurried outside.

Drenched from head to toe, Mizu's rapid breathing calmed as he looked up at the sprinklers and smiled. The water made him feel much better.

"I'm not sure how it all happened, but the water saved me just at the right time," he muttered as he opened his eyes on the beach. "Oh, well," he sighed, looking out at the ocean. "Still no waves. Today I need to surf more than ever, but I guess it's just destined to be a bad day."

Saying it out loud made him feel a bit better, so he kept right on going—no matter how weird it might sound to anyone else. "This is the only place where I feel I belong. No one understands me, how I feel, or who I am. I know I'm not like the other kids at school, and no one seems to think I'm cool. I know being different isn't bad, so why does it

Facing the Drought

make me feel so sad? I wish I knew why they don't like me and always laugh at me. If they would just see past the science stuff, then they would understand what a good friend I could be."

MIZU'S SONG
**I AM A DIFFERENT**

*PLAY* this song at
TheSuperSustainables.com

Fifteen Years Later

He sighed and rested his head on his arms, moving it from side to side and trying to keep his temper under control. Then he suddenly didn't care anymore. He grabbed two handfuls of sand and flung them away. Then he moved down the sand until he was sitting at the water's edge looking out at the ocean, and still there were no surfing waves. He rested his head on his knees and splashed his feet about in the water as it rolled up his ankles. He was incredibly restless and couldn't sit still. As the next wave passed over his feet, he wriggled them around in irritation. *Grrrrrr, I need a wave, like now!* he thought as he banged his head lightly on his knees.

When he looked up Mizu got the biggest shock of his life. A gigantic wave hurtled toward him. Mizu tried to scramble to his feet, but he wasn't fast enough. The wave knocked him down and sent his surfboard sailing off down the beach. He choked on the water as he struggled to get upright, then looked around at the people on the beach, thinking that he needed to warn everyone. But nobody seemed to have noticed what had happened.

Mizu wasn't exactly sure himself, as the ocean was now as flat and calm as it had been a moment before.

He jogged over to where his surfboard had been tossed and picked it up, looking back out at the horizon. *What on earth just happened?* he thought. The scientist in him wrestled with what his eyes had just seen, but there didn't seem to be an explanation. He sat down on the sand a bit further up the beach, completely lost in thought. After a few minutes, the jarring sound of a loud alarm snapped him out of his thoughts and back to reality. *Beep, beep, beep.*

He looked down at his top-of-the-line diving watch, which he'd received for his birthday after begging his parents to buy it for him. It was loaded with features—a list as long as his arm—all of which he knew how to use. After water and science, gadgets were something he just couldn't live without. Now he remembered he'd set an alarm so that he wouldn't lose track of time, which he often did. Part of the deal he had made with his folks when they agreed to buy him such an extravagant birthday gift was that he would never be late getting home again. Mizu's father was unbending about "never!"

This particular alarm reminded him that he needed to head home, as it was time for his online science meeting. He was part of a science discussion blog and often chatted with other science-minded teens from around the world about new discoveries and cutting-edge technologies. He had less than an hour to make it home, so he gathered up his board and headed over to get his towel. As he walked, he happened to notice a girl about his age walking determinedly across the sand, picking up all the trash littering the beach.

*Wow*, he thought, *you don't see that every day. I guess I'm not the only kid in Santa Monica who isn't at the game.*

He wished he had the guts to go over and talk to her and tell her how much he admired what she was doing, but he was too shy and had never been very good at talking to girls. They usually thought he was kind of nerdy, and never really took him seriously, especially when he spoke to them about science stuff. As the girl walked past him, she looked up and their eyes met briefly. But by the time he realized he should smile, wave, or say hello, she had passed him by, absorbed in her task.

As Mizu gathered his things and prepared to head home, he looked back at the girl and said out loud, "Yeah, the world needs more people like you!"

Chapter 3

# The Voice

Mother Nature watched from above and smiled. She had been patient for 15 long years, but the time for action had finally come...

• • • •

It was the final moments of the fourth quarter, and Franco had already thrown three touchdown passes. The fans were screaming and cheering for him. He had to be honest—he really loved the attention. And what he loved even *more* was that he seemed to have caught the eye of one of the cheerleaders from the other team. He watched her between quarters when they performed their routines, and thought she was really pretty. *I'll have to find a way to talk to her after the game*, he vowed at halftime. *Hopefully she won't be too upset that we are going to defeat her team.*

But as he dropped back to throw one more touchdown pass—which would secure the victory—he heard a soft, echoing voice. In his surprise and confusion, he threw an interception.

"Franco!" screamed the coach. "Now is not the time to daydream! Get it together out there!"

Franco, who'd watched in shock as the safety from the other team grabbed the ball, suddenly regained his focus and realized that the safety had fumbled when he was tackled, and his own running back had recovered. *Whew!* he thought. The game was close and there wasn't much time left on the clock. There was still a chance to win!

But then, just as he dropped back, he heard the voice again.

*"Franco! Franco! Meet me at the totem pole in Palisades Park at*

*noon tomorrow to find out your purpose on this earth."*

Franco shook his head to clear his thoughts. He looked around and saw nobody that the voice could possibly belong to, even though he had heard it so clearly. No, no, no! Hearing voices nobody else seemed to hear was never a good sign—he knew that much—and yet there was something so familiar about the voice. Something almost… comforting. He seemed to recognize it from somewhere.

Luckily, he'd thrown the ball before he stopped to think about the voice. The roar of the crowd brought him back, and he realized that his receiver had caught the pass—and that they'd won the game. His teammates scooped him up on their shoulders to carry him off the field, whooping and cheering in victory.

*Maybe I've just been running around out in the sun too long,* Franco thought. He pushed the voice out of his head so he could enjoy the victory celebration with his team. He craned his head above the crowd to look for the cheerleader he wanted to meet but couldn't seem to find her.

• • • •

Arielle knew she was looking good. She had done her hair up with pretty clips for the big game, and was pleased that she had received quite a few admiring glances from the boys—as well as some jealous glares from the girls. She had also caught the other team's quarterback staring at her more than once.

Now, near the end of the game, though, things were getting serious. Their team was about to lose, so the squad pulled out all the stops to cheer them on. They lined up along the side of the field and waved their pom-poms, shouted, and cheered—they had just a few seconds left and needed another touchdown to win. Arielle launched herself into a backwards somersault and, as she landed, suddenly heard a voice.

*"Arielle! Arielle! Meet me at the totem pole in Palisades Park at noon tomorrow to find out your purpose on this earth."*

Arielle stopped and looked around in confusion. Lots of people surrounded her, but they were all shouting and screaming and focusing on the game. No, she was sure the voice couldn't possibly belong to anyone near her.

"Hey, Arielle," Sarah shouted, noticing her friend standing absolutely still when everyone else was jumping around and screaming. "What's wrong?"

Arielle realized she must look a bit strange, so she wiped the blank look off her face and quickly rejoined her friend. "Nothing," she replied, with what she hoped was a convincing smile. "Just totally bummed our team lost!"

As they walked off the field, Arielle couldn't shake the feeling that she had heard that voice somewhere before.

● ● ● ●

Tara wiped her brow as she tied a knot in the top of the last bag of garbage. *Three full bags today,* she thought. *That's quite a haul. People are so careless!* She took the bags over to the trash bins at the end of the beach. As she shoved the last one in, a lone seagull dropped onto the edge of the bin and let out a loud squawk.

"Yeah, I know," Tara replied automatically. "But it's all clean now. No more danger to you and your friends. I'll be back again next week."

The seagull ruffled his feathers and squawked again before flying off. Tara smiled. It was nice to feel as if someone was grateful for her efforts, even if it was just one seagull. As she stood looking out over the horizon, she suddenly heard someone speaking.

*"Tara! Tara! Meet me at the totem pole in Palisades Park at noon tomorrow to find out your purpose on this earth."*

She spun around quickly, but there was nobody there. *A seagull?* Tara thought, but shook her head at the idea. "Obviously a seagull isn't talking to me," she berated herself. She must still be on edge from when she'd thought the squirrel was talking to her. Plus, she had been so upset lately about what she had seen people doing to the earth that she spent a lot of time up in her tree. "First squirrels, now seagulls. I have got to get a grip," she said.

*That must be it,* she thought. *I need to get some human company soon, before I go completely crazy!*

She chuckled to herself as she headed home, determined not to visit the squirrels for at least a week.

● ● ● ●

Mizu entered his room and shut the door behind him. He propped his surfboard against the closet and turned on his iMac, which had been programmed to greet him. Then he flopped down on his bed, opened a group chat on his phone, and relaxed while waiting for the other kids. That's when he heard the voice.

*"Mizu! Mizu! Meet me at the totem pole in Palisades Park at noon tomorrow to find out your purpose on this earth."*

At first it didn't quite register. Then his iMac burst to life with, "Hey Mizu, how was your day?" He bolted upright.

"What was *that?!*" he asked loudly. "Hello? Who's there?"

No reply.

As his phone started signaling the arrival of his chat group friends, he settled back against his pillow, thinking it was funny that he didn't feel scared of the voice he had heard. But he didn't give it much more thought as he opened the first chat window and joined the discussion about chemical reactions and carbon emissions.

## Chapter 4
## Enlightenment

The next morning dawned bright and sunny as Arielle, Mizu, Franco, and Tara all woke up thinking about the voice they had heard the previous day. And though they didn't understand it, they each knew exactly where they would be at noon.

● ● ● ●

Promptly at noon, the four approached the totem pole, coming from different directions until they were positioned around the pole at each of the compass points. They eyed each other warily, none of them quite sure what to think. Franco, who never let a little awkwardness stand in his way, broke the silence by turning to Arielle and saying, "You're the flying cheerleader from the big game yesterday, aren't you?"

"And you're the quarterback," she replied, flashing her baby-blue eyes at him while adjusting her purple backpack into a more comfortable position.

They turned to look at the other two. Tara was the first to speak up.

"Well, I wasn't at the game," she said, looking at Mizu.

"Me neither," he replied. He was far too shy and embarrassed to say he recognized Tara from the beach, especially when she didn't seem to have any clue who he was. He kept his mouth shut.

They all seemed ready to say something, but stalled, as if they weren't sure how to begin. Finally, Franco said what everyone else was thinking.

"I heard a voice telling me to be here at noon. What about you guys?"

The other three instantly relaxed and jumped in with a chorus of "Me, too!" They all began to smile and look at each other in more friendly ways, as if they'd realized that they were in it together—whatever "it" was.

"What on earth do you think this is all about?" Tara asked. "And where are all the people who are usually in the park at noon on a Saturday?"

The others looked around and noticed for the first time that the park seemed strangely devoid of its normal weekend hustle and bustle. As they puzzled over this, a shadow suddenly passed over them.

"#WhoBlocksTheSun?" asked Arielle. "There wasn't a cloud in the sky two minutes ago."

They all tilted their heads upwards and saw something floating down from the sky, completely blocking the sun. As it got closer and closer, the light from the sun beamed out and seemed to glow brighter than they had ever seen before. They shielded their eyes from the glare, until the mysterious floating object landed and they saw that it was a woman. She was so beautiful that all they could do was stare.

"Hello," the woman greeted them. "I am so glad to see all four of you here. My name is Mother Nature, and I have called you here for a very special reason."

Franco burst out with, "Mother Nature? What, are you going to tell us a nursery rhyme?"

Arielle replied, "No, silly, that's Mother Goose!" She twisted her mouth at him, as if she'd never heard anything quite so stupid.

Ever the practical scientist, Mizu exclaimed, "Mother Nature? That's not possible!" He was a little shocked at the sound of his own voice—but also shocked at what he was seeing before him, and who this woman claimed to be.

"Oh, I assure you that it is very possible, for here I stand before you, about to ask you to undertake a mission of extreme urgency and importance. Please sit here on the benches and allow me to explain," Mother Nature said softly.

The kids all realized this was definitely the voice they'd heard the day before. The one that they'd all thought sounded so comforting and familiar, which was odd, since none of them had ever talked to this woman before.

# Enlightenment

"It all began here in this park, 15 years ago. I placed the spirits of the four elements—earth, air, fire and water—into you before you were even born."

The kids were mesmerized by the strangely beautiful woman, but that didn't mean that any of them believed her...yet.

"All life on earth is dependent on these four elements," Mother Nature continued. "And each one has special properties that show themselves in different ways. Water has magnetic properties, and without it we could not exist. It is the source of all life. Fire has electrical and creative properties, and it too is vital for survival. Air contains oxygen that is essential for all living beings, if they want to breathe. It's invisible, yet very powerful, for it allows fire and water to coexist. And the element of earth binds everything together so the planet can thrive. All four elements are completely interwoven, and none can exist without the others."

They were stunned when she added, "It is from these elements that you will draw your strength for the tasks ahead. For the four of you are very special, and have been chosen by me to help save the earth from more abuse and neglect."

"Save the earth? Really? Are you for real?" asked Arielle with a giggle.

Tara shot Arielle a look of disapproval and thought, *Who is this girl and why is she so rude and disrespectful?* She tried to stay calm, though, as she looked at Mother Nature and asked, "Why us? Why here? What's so special about this park?"

"It's not the park that's special — it's this totem pole," replied Mother Nature. She gestured to the tall pole a few feet away from them.

"That ugly thing?" asked Arielle, scrunching up her nose in disgust.

Tara looked over at the cheerleader again with exasperation. "Totem poles are full of mystery. The animals all mean different things, don't they?" she said, looking over at the mysterious and radiant woman.

"Yes, you are quite right, Tara," Mother Nature replied with a smile.

"Hey, how did you know my name?" Tara asked with surprise.

"I know everything about you. I have been waiting a long time for the day when you could finally begin to fulfill your destinies. That day has finally come."

"Okay, I don't know about the rest of you, but I'm, like, starting to totally freak out!" Arielle blurted, looking somewhat panicked. "This weird lady's been watching us? Really? And none of you think that's… strange?"

"There's no need to be afraid, Arielle," Mother Nature said kindly. "Let me explain this to you properly."

The teens sat listening, wide-eyed, as Mother Nature told them the tale of the earth's great sadness, and how the planet had summoned her and brought her to life through her own energy. She told them how she had seen abuse and neglect wherever she went on the earth, and realized she needed human help to make the necessary changes. She told them how she had chosen their mothers in the park, all those years ago, and how she had watched with pride as they each grew since then.

"So what's so special about this totem pole, then?" Franco asked. "And what exactly are we supposed to do with… well, whatever it is you say you've given us?"

"Well," said Mother Nature, "totem poles are the talk of legends and are shrouded in myth and mystery. What you see depends on what your beliefs are, which makes it the perfect object for my purposes. What nobody knows is that on New Year's Day, 1926, an enormous undersea volcano threatened to erupt in the Pacific Ocean—one so fierce that it would have obliterated life on the entire planet. I managed to get it under control with the help of the element spirits that I keep here in my necklace.

However, due to its sheer strength, it will forevermore pose a threat to the earth. I needed a plan. I commissioned this totem pole from the local Indians, and when it was completed, I placed the spirits of the four elements inside the pole to stand as a beacon of power. You see, the volcano is not far from here. This was the closest point I could find—a place for the pole to stand and keep watch over the earth without alarming the people, who have always thought it just a gift. Now that you are of age, it is time to perform the ritual that will bring your powers to life and completely bind you to your elements. Are you all ready?"

Without waiting for a response, she continued. "Please join hands to complete the circle."

"Huh-uh, no way am I holding hands with people I don't know. #SoGross," Arielle said, stepping forward and flicking her long blonde hair over her shoulder. "This has to be some kind of joke, right?"

"This is no joke, Arielle," Mother Nature said with a grave voice. "The situation is actually very serious."

"No, what the situation is, is ridiculous," Arielle shouted back, stomping her foot for added emphasis. "This is just unreal. You float down out of the sky and tell us we have to save the earth. That kind of stuff only happens in movies or dreams. So here we go, everybody, I am going to wake myself up from this dream. Goodbye, it was nice to meet you all," she said as she slapped herself on the cheek. "Ouch, that hurt. Wake up, wake up, Arielle!" she repeated as she slapped herself again.

Mother Nature had never imagined it would be this difficult to get them to believe her. She opened her mouth to respond, but before she could get any words out, Arielle burst out with, "OMG are you still all here? #ThingsThatFreakMeOut."

Then, after a short pause to process the situation, she slapped her hand on her forehead and went on. "Oh now I get it, I know what this is. We're on one of those hidden camera reality shows, right? We're going to be on TV." She started fixing her hair and straightening her clothes and plastered a megawatt smile on her face. "I always thought those things were staged. Why didn't we get a heads up? I would have picked out a much cuter outfit for my TV debut."

The other kids watched how Arielle overreacted and Tara, finally losing her patience, snapped, "Arielle, I don't know you, but get yourself together. What you're saying is the most ridiculous thing I've ever heard!" She snorted with disdain, then looked over at Mizu for support and rolled her eyes.

Mizu, who was still stunned into speechlessness, didn't feel comfortable around these new kids or the situation. He just smiled weakly back at her.

"Okay, Curly," Arielle snapped back at Tara. "Do you have a better explanation for what's going on here? If so, do share it with us."

Tara glared at Arielle and demanded, "Stop freaking out! Mother Nature is trying to tell us why she brought us all here. So be quiet and let her talk!"

"Don't tell me what to do, *Curly*," said Arielle with her hands on her hips.

"My name is Tara!" she responded through gritted teeth.

"Take it easy, *chicas*," said Franco as he stepped forward to stand between them. "Arielle, you stay here and relax, and Tara, you go over there. This is not the time to lose your tempers."

Turning to Mother Nature, he continued, "I really respect who you say you are, but all of this seems kind of unreal. How do we know you're not the ghost of an old witch who died long ago and is looking for fresh blood to keep you young-looking, or something to that effect? I've seen some creepy movies like that. I don't know about you guys, but I'm leaving before it's too late and she hypnotizes all of us." Franco turned and started to walk away.

"Hold on!" screamed Arielle. "I don't want a witch to drink my blood! #SoCreepy. Don't leave me alone with her. I'm coming with you." She followed his lead, both of them in a hurry to get out of there.

A voice murmured, "Well, I believe her." It was Mizu.

Franco and Arielle stopped and looked at him.

"Oh, so you *are* alive," said Arielle. "I thought she already turned you into a zombie."

"What did you say?" asked Franco.

"I believe Mother Nature," repeated Mizu in a slightly louder voice.

"What? You believe that she's an old witch?" Arielle asked with a giggle as she squinted at him.

"Maybe you can stop talking for a second and give him a chance to talk," Tara said tersely to Arielle.

Arielle shot a look back at Tara. "Who does she think she is?" she mumbled to herself.

"Please," Tara said kindly, "explain what you mean."

"Okay … My name's Mizu, and I have to admit that something weird happened to me the other day when I was at the beach."

"Weird things happen to weird people—everybody knows that!

Let's go, Franco," Arielle interrupted.

"Shh, Arielle. Let him finish," insisted Franco.

Arielle crossed her arms and rolled her eyes, but let Mizu continue.

"I was sitting on the sand," Mizu said, "and feeling down because I couldn't surf. There were no waves, see. I was looking at the sand, when suddenly a huge wave appeared. Before I could get away, it washed ashore and knocked me over. I was in total shock because I didn't know where it came from. When I finally stood up, the sea was calm again—no more waves. It was really bizarre and it felt like something powerful made it happen, but I didn't know what it was."

The others listened attentively to Mizu's story with wide eyes.

"Well," Mother Nature stepped up and said calmly. "It's true, Mizu. Your power over water created that wave. But you wouldn't have known that at the time. Your strong emotions brought it out."

It dawned on Mizu that perhaps his connection with water had "activated" the sprinklers at school during his altercation with Dylan. But he decided to keep this thought to himself.

Mother Nature continued, "I'm sure if all of you think carefully, each of you has recently experienced some strange happenings you couldn't quite explain. This was because of your hidden powers. You see, sometimes the element is too strong to be suppressed, and it shows itself before it is formally activated."

"O-M-G!" Arielle interrupted. "Yeah, something weird did happen to me. The other day I saw a cyclone underneath me and like, I really thought I was flying …"

She trailed off, realizing what she had just blurted out to a bunch of strangers. She would just die if this secret got out. She would lose all her followers on Instagram and become a social outcast at school.

# Enlightenment

Her cheeks started to burn with embarrassment, but before she could jump in to do damage control, Franco interrupted.

"Oh right, now that I think about it, I thought I saw fire come out of my fingers the other day. It was … weird. And definitely unexplained."

"I thought I heard a squirrel talk," Tara admitted hesitantly.

"These are exactly the kind of things I'm talking about. Before you were even born, you received these special abilities, and if you think about it, you are all very gifted in many ways," said Mother Nature.

This helped to put them all at ease about what they had just confided to her and each other, and once again the kids started feeling as if they were truly in this together.

"These abilities are showing themselves in these strange ways because it is time. The longer we wait, the harder they will be to conceal, so it's time to learn what you are, what you can do, and how to control and use your powers. From now on, you will be *real heroes* and responsible for saving the earth! Your purpose is to educate people on how to live a more sustainable lifestyle and preserve the precious resources on our beautiful planet."

Mizu looked at Mother Nature with concern and asked, "But how are we going to do that? There's only the four of us against the entire world. And who will listen to us? We're just kids!"

"You will be far from 'just kids' in a few moments," Mother Nature told them. "If we are to be successful on our mission, we have to get our message out to other kids. You and millions like you are the future of our planet. If we don't change the mindset of the young, our earth will certainly be damaged beyond repair, and this will have a negative effect on future generations. We have to hope that by educating children, we will help adults who have been so irresponsible to see the error in their ways and change their bad habits before it's too late. Remember, Mizu, change begins with a single action—and no action is too small to make a difference.

"You are all smart kids," she continued. "That's why you were chosen. So I'm asking you now to just take a moment to think and listen to me. Think about what I have told you and about what you have seen and experienced in the recent weeks with your abilities coming to the surface. Is there any other logical explanation for why you are sprouting fire from your fingers, conjuring cyclones in the gym, hearing squirrels speak, or creating waves on the beach?"

The four kids looked at one another, confused, but realizing that if what Mother Nature said was true, she was about to turn them into heroes with special powers. This seemed like a fantasy…but the truth was that each of them also knew what they had seen and felt over the previous weeks.

And those things didn't feel normal. They felt…heroic.

# Enlightenment

Chapter 5

# The Ritual

Mother Nature saw their resolve starting to weaken, and turned to address them again. "You are right to be concerned and question me. After all, I am a complete stranger who appeared in your lives out of nowhere. I know you live in a dangerous world where you need to be careful of some people. But I am not one of them. I promise you that. Now, I want you all to think about how you felt when you heard my voice speaking to you. Were any of you frightened?"

They looked at each other, each a bit nervous to be the first to admit that they hadn't been scared. Surprised, yes. But not afraid.

Mother Nature smiled again. "Exactly," she said. "And are any of you frightened now?"

After a long pause, where they all looked around at each other again, Franco said, "Well, I for one am not frightened. Just wary because this all sounds so far-fetched."

Mother Nature nodded. "I'm going to ask you all to do something now," she said. "I know this sounds unbelievable, but I think we can all agree that you are not in any danger." She looked at them expectantly, and when no one responded—or disagreed with her—she continued.

"So I am going to ask you all to simply trust me. Even though there is no scientific evidence of what I'm telling you. And even though it seems totally unreal. Just trust me. Let me do the ritual. Nobody is going to be hurt, I promise. I'm just going to activate your powers and give you the ability to control them. Then you will see that all I've been telling you is true."

Arielle stared at this mystical woman, confused, but had to admit she was starting to feel more relaxed and more comfortable with what Mother Nature was saying. *If it's all true then I will have real powers, kind of like Wonder Woman,* she thought. *That will be pretty cool.* She imagined her life as a famous hero, then stepped forward exclaiming, "Okay, I'm in. #ClaimToFame."

"It's not going to be all fame and fortune, Arielle," Mother Nature warned. "You have a long, hard road ahead of you, and the message you will deliver will not always make you popular. People can be very set in their ways and resistant to change. So it will be a big challenge for all of you."

Franco, not wanting to seem like a coward in front of the girl he was trying to impress, stepped forward and said, "Okay, what the heck, I'm in too." His gut told him to trust this being. If he was truly honest, he would have to admit he felt a connection with her—one that he couldn't really explain. And since he'd spent his entire life trusting his instincts, this didn't seem like the time to stop.

Besides, the idea of being a hero sounded kind of cool.

He used this as an excuse to grab Arielle's hand and pull her forward to stand closer to the totem pole with him. Closer to where Mother Nature was.

*Well at least if nothing comes of this, I will have gotten to hold her hand,* he thought. *She might even agree to go on a date with me.*

Mizu, on the other hand, was having a wrestling match inside his head. He thought everything there was to be known about the world could be explained by science. This was a leap of faith, with no evidence at all, and he was really scared. But he also had a deep desire to belong—to fit in somewhere and find his place in the world. Could this be his chance? Could this be the group that would finally accept him and make him feel welcome?

And if they were saving the world at the same time…what could be better?

In the end, his longing to be part of a group and maybe develop true friendships with these three strangers won, and Mizu stepped forward without saying a word and took Arielle's free hand.

Arielle looked pointedly at Tara. *So I guess I need to work with Curly,* she thought. She didn't think there was room on the team for two girls, and would have loved to be the center of attention, with two boys helping her out. In fact, she realized, she was mildly irritated with Mother Nature for including Tara in the first place. But then she gave Tara a once-over from head to toe and took note of her earth-tone pants with the floral print, t-shirt, and curly hair with a flower tucked behind her ear. *No need to be worried,* she thought with a twist of her mouth. *No way can she ever outshine me.*

Tara, on the other hand, prided herself on being logical and always making sound, levelheaded decisions. She didn't like to let emotion rule. But even she had to admit that curiosity had gotten the best of her. And Mother Nature had said something truly appealing to her— they would be doing what was best for the earth. Wasn't that what she'd been building her life on, anyhow? So how could this change anything? She stepped forward and joined hands with Mizu and Franco, then turned to Mother Nature and said, "Okay, I think we're ready, Mother Nature. Now what?"

Mother Nature breathed a sigh of relief. These four were stronger than she had thought. She hadn't expected them to put up such a fight, and at one point thought all was lost, that the four of them were going to walk away. And that she would have to explain to Earth that after 15 long years of patience, her plan had failed. But now she realized that her heroes had just been taking their time to think it through and make sure that this was right.

They were heroes, after all—they had to be certain they were doing this for the right reasons. And now she knew they were.

She took a moment to compose herself, then stepped into the middle of the circle. She placed her right hand on the totem pole and walked slowly around the inside of the circle, placing her hand on each of their joined hands as she went. The four kids experienced a sudden warmth enveloping their hands, and then it felt almost as if their hands had become glued together. Mother Nature smiled as she saw their hands begin to glow golden where they were joined. The bond was forming, just as she had planned. As she watched, the glow began to extend into a circle around her heroes, and she chanted:

*These four young heroes unite as one,*
*Led by me, descendant of sky and sun.*
*Together we fight to reclaim our earth,*
*And help people see just how much it's worth.*
*Release your spirits and grant us your powers,*
*Let strength and wisdom now become ours.*

As she spoke, she rubbed her necklace, taking care to rub each of the four jewels four times in a circular motion. A colorful stream of mist shot out of each jewel, slithering through the air like the tail of a kite. The four streams danced in the air around the totem pole faster and faster, and it started to glow as if a bright spotlight was directly above it. Then the streams entered the totem pole from the top and the glow disappeared.

The teens looked on in complete fascination, not having any idea what had just happened.

Within moments, the pole released the full powers of the elements. A force field seemed to surround it—it was nothing that could be seen, but they all could feel its power. Suddenly four glowing orbs the size of bowling balls launched from the top of the pole and sailed down toward each of them. One orb soared to a spot in front of Franco. Another floated over to Mizu. A third spun around in front of Tara. And the last one hovered in front of Arielle.

They continued to stare in amazement.

"Look at your orb and feel its power," Mother Nature instructed. "In a few moments, the powers in the orbs will connect to each of you and become a part of you, making you special — much like your DNA does."

Nobody dared to move or speak. They were transfixed by the ritual, and none of them wanted to break the spell.

As they watched in amazement, four long silver lights started beaming out of Mother Nature's fingers. As thin as dental floss, they glowed as if they were charged with electricity. One straight silver spoke extended toward each of the kids and attached to the orbs. Then, as Mother Nature raised her hand toward the sky, each spoke lifted, taking the orbs with them until they came together in the sky, directly above the totem pole. When the four orbs touched, the electricity from the silver spokes seemed to create an energy field around them, until a larger silver orb surrounded the four smaller ones—almost like an elastic band holding them together. Then the larger silver orb started to spin around, faster and faster...until it was just a big blur of light.

Mother Nature chanted her verse one last time while all the orbs spun together. Then she threw her hands upwards and sent the orbs catapulting high up into the air until they were just small dots, barely visible.

All four kids looked upwards, wondering what could possibly

happen next. They watched wide-eyed as the orbs fell back down to earth as fast as they had risen. Arielle wondered briefly if they were going to land on their heads—and if it would hurt or leave a bump. Even in the middle of such a serious, life-changing experience, she was worried about her appearance.

But she'd worried for nothing because the four orbs came to a peaceful halt just above their heads and emitted a glow, encircling each of them with their powers. The power of water for Mizu, fire for Franco, air for Arielle, and earth for Tara.

While nobody spoke, each felt warm and comforted by the glowing light. They each instinctively turned their faces toward the source of the light, closing their eyes and breathing deeply as if they were trying to absorb every last beam of light into their bodies. It was the most wonderful feeling any of them had ever felt.

And then it was over. Mother Nature snapped her fingers and each orb shot down and entered their hosts through their hearts, causing them to momentarily lose their breath from the force.

Mother Nature looked to them and said, "While you walk the earth as individuals, you are also now united by a bond so powerful that nothing can break it. The power of four has been activated. Go forth with confidence and use your powers wisely to make the earth healthy once again."

Tara was the first to speak up. "But what does that mean? What are these powers and how are we going to control them?"

Arielle, with a look of suspicion on her face, actually agreed with Tara. "Yeah. While that was a pretty cool ritual, I don't really feel any different."

"You guys are an impatient bunch, aren't you?" Mother Nature said with a smile. "I still have a little more to explain to each of you about why you were chosen for this mission. Let's start with you, Arielle. The raven at the top of the totem pole holds the essence of air. Arielle, you have a strong personality and know exactly what you want. You have a passion for fashion and a keen eye for detail. With this talent you will connect to the people you meet and get them to imitate what you do, which is vital for this mission. You are a natural leader with a love of learning. People will be drawn to you and follow your example, and this will enable you to show them the right way to do things. You are often inspired with great ideas and never afraid to question things that don't seem right. Change does not scare you, if you can see that it makes sense. This element fits your personality well, and that is why you were chosen."

For once, Arielle was speechless, so Mother Nature continued. "Arielle, you will be responsible for helping people understand how to keep the air clean enough for us to breathe."

As Arielle nodded her agreement, her backpack started to squirm around and make a strange squeaking sound. Startled, she jumped and quickly wriggled out of it, dropping it and just managing to stop herself from stomping on it. #WhatonEarth? How did a mouse get into my bag? she thought as she shuddered from the grossness of thinking about a rodent in her bag, crawling all over her things.

But then the backpack shouted out, "Hey, let me out. It's so dark in here."

Arielle stared wide-eyed at her sparkly purple bag, which was now moving around on the ground…and talking.

"Don't be alarmed Arielle," Mother Nature said. "Open the bag."

Arielle reached down with shaking fingers and unzipped her backpack. She let out a shriek of surprise when she saw that it was her stuffed toy bird, Birdie, hopping around. She jumped out of the bag and ruffled her feathers, clearly no longer just an inanimate toy.

"It's about time," squawked Birdie. Looking at Arielle's shocked face, she quickly hopped up onto her shoulder and gave her ear an affectionate nibble. "It's so dark and cramped in that bag where you

keep me hidden all the time. It's good to be out in the fresh air and sunshine…don't look so worried," Birdie continued as she stretched her wings and took off to circle above them. "I'm still your best friend. But I can talk back now."

"Wow, a talking bird. This is cool!" exclaimed Franco.

Mizu remained quiet, trying to figure out what just happened—and how.

"What's a live bird doing in your bag, Arielle?" demanded Tara. "You could have killed her."

She was really mad at this point — maybe angrier than she should have been—because she had no tolerance for people who abused animals. Because it was Arielle — who she'd decided she didn't care for — made it even worse. What was this girl thinking, keeping a bird in her bag like that?

An embarrassed Arielle shot her an angry glare, refusing to dignify such a question with an answer. She gave everyone a nervous smile as her brain tried to make sense of what had just happened and how she was going to explain it to them. Couldn't everyone else tell that Birdie wasn't a real bird?

Maybe not, she realized, as she looked at the bird flying over her head. The stuffed animal had somehow become real.

#MostEmbarrassingMomentOfMyLife, she thought to herself. "B-b-but how?" she asked aloud. "How did you turn her into a real bird that talks? Are you a w-w-witch after all?" Birdie perched on her shoulder and stared her in the face. Arielle looked back and forth from Birdie to Mother Nature, completely confused.

"I am not a witch," Mother Nature replied with a smile. "This was not my doing, but rather yours. You see," she continued, "Birdie is your truest friend. She is the one thing you have never been able to do without, and it has been that way since the moment you got her as a gift. She has been your best friend since the day you were born and has never been far from where you are. This power—the power of love—turned her into a real bird."

*Oh okay, that's sweet,* Tara thought, relieved and a little ashamed of her accusation.

Arielle was just staring, though, so Birdie pecked her on the ear, and said, "Hey, snap out of it. You can stop hiding me away now! I for one am getting tired of being crammed into lockers and bags!" She stretched out her wings and flapped them for effect.

Mother Nature looked at Birdie reproachfully. "That's enough, Birdie," she said. "Give her a break. It's a lot to absorb all at once."

Arielle looked at Birdie, still in shock that she was really flying and talking, and asked, "How on earth am I going to explain having a talking bird to people? Birdie doesn't exactly look like a parrot or mockingbird—or anything anyone has ever seen before. No one's going to believe I suddenly have a pet bird. One that *talks*."

Mother Nature reassured her, "You don't have to worry. You four are exceptional, and your special powers let you hear Birdie's sounds as words. To everyone else, Birdie will look and sound like a normal bird—only you four will be able to understand her."

*Gosh, I wish my pets could talk like Birdie,* Tara thought. *But it doesn't really matter, because we understand each other so well.* She smiled at the thought, but couldn't help wondering what her superpower would give her.

Mother Nature continued, "Birdie is right, though. You don't have to hide her anymore. She will be with you to help fulfill your destiny. Always keep her close by so you never get into trouble—she'll help you get out of any scrape."

"I always do."

"Oh, one more thing Arielle," Mother Nature said.

"How can there possibly be more?" Arielle was used to playing it cool and not letting her true feelings show, but this was an awful lot to take in and she wasn't sure how much more she would be able to handle without some sort of anxiety attack.

"Well," said Mother Nature with a smile, "you also have the ability to fly."

Arielle let out a shriek of excitement and clapped her hands together. "Me? Fly? Like Birdie? #WhatAnAwesomeSuperPower! Am I going to get wings now?"

Mother Nature was glad to see at least one of the four looking a bit more enthusiastic about the whole hero thing. "Well, not quite like Birdie. You won't have wings, because you don't need them—you are now fully connected to your element. Because your element is air, all you have to do is think of yourself flying and it will happen. When you activate your powers, you'll glide through the air as easily as if you were the wind. It will allow you and Birdie to work together in times of need."

Mother Nature turned to Mizu. "The water element is represented by the fish, and it belongs to you, Mizu. This element is perfectly suited to you because, besides being very clever, you have a caring soul that feels things deeply. However, you have taught yourself to control and hide your emotions and rarely show people your true feelings.

"You are very sensitive—your heart is your guide in everything you do, and as a result you are very empathetic to other people's experiences, and compassionate to all. You give and love with everything you've got because you have an instinct for caretaking. Also, you love to learn new things, invent new technologies, and bring your imaginative ideas to life. The sky is the limit for you, and when you're passionate about something, you give it your all. And it usually works out how you wish. You make a point of being easygoing and are drawn to mysterious things that cannot be easily explained."

Mizu could only stare. *How does she know all that?*

"All these traits belong to you, Mizu," Mother Nature said with a knowing smile. "You will be responsible for teaching people how to conserve water, our most precious and important resource. When necessary, you'll have the power to control water, including storms, tsunamis, and floods. And most important, you now have the ability to breathe underwater.

"Mizu," she continued, "your element wields the most power, and I have chosen it for you because I know you are sensible enough to handle such a big responsibility."

Mizu was touched that Mother Nature would place so much confidence in him. Finally, *someone* understood his true value and pointed it out without ridiculing him! But that didn't mean he knew how to respond. Instead, he just stared at her in awe, wondering what exactly he was supposed to say to that. Control the water? *Breathe* underwater? How was it possible?

Mother Nature turned to Tara. "You, too, Tara, are a special soul, so the bear represents you. It symbolizes the power of the earth and the need for healing. You are not a dreamer, and you have realistic expectations for your life. You love the adventure of travel and exploring the nature and cultures of the places you visit. Animals are important to you and you have a special bond with them. In fact, I think you sometimes feel more connected to animals than to people! You really want to make a difference in the world, and your giving nature means you often put others before yourself."

While Tara tried to digest this, Mother Nature continued. "You are responsible for helping people understand the effects of climate change and how to respect the earth. The source of your powers comes from the special seed you planted in your yard."

"Wait...my seed?" Tara asked, amazed. She'd known it was special, but didn't think it was *that* special.

"That's right, Tara, the seed you planted in your garden."

"But how do you know about that?" Tara asked, perplexed and confused beyond belief. "Not even my parents know about that seed."

"I left that seed especially for you. Just continue nurturing and caring for it. It will provide your strength and power."

Tara nodded, feeling a little bit let down that she didn't get an animal like Arielle. She really liked that special plant, but...

"That's not all," Mother Nature continued. "You will be sensitive to things that happen on the earth—whether good or bad—and accordingly, you will be able to calm the earth when it gets angry. That means you will have the ability to control earthquakes, landslides, and volcanoes. You will also be able to communicate with all the earth's animals. I have placed a great responsibility on you, Tara, and I know you are up for the challenge."

Tara looked Mother Nature straight in the eye and said, "You can count on me. I won't let you down."

Lastly, Mother Nature turned to Franco, who was anxiously waiting to hear about his new abilities. "You are passionate, exciting, and intense, and this is why the wolf is for you, Franco. You are not concerned with accomplishments or possessions, but rather inspired by the very experience of life. You are a charismatic leader and handle yourself well in front of an audience, and inside you have the soul of an artist who likes to decorate the world with your creations. You are a loyal friend and true to yourself. You are full of dreams, and always follow your heart, even if it means 'playing with fire' or trying new things. Problems don't get you down—you attack them head on. The wolf is as ferocious as fire and, just like the wolf, the spirit of fire will run freely within you as you become one with the flames."

Franco responded with a grin. "A fire wolf—I like it!"

"There's more," continued Mother Nature. "Your mission is to teach others about fire safety and using fire responsibly. You will be able to control fires and protect others from it as well. And you'll have the ability to jump high and soar through the air."

"Seriously?" Franco asked in astonishment, his eyes growing as big as saucers. "You mean I can fly like Ironman?"

Mother Nature winked and said, "I don't know this 'Ironman' you speak of, but if he flies, then yes, you will be able to fly as well."

Mother Nature looked at her four heroes and continued, "Now you are real heroes with unique powers, and each of you needs to learn how to use and control them. The manifestation of your powers is dependent on how you have absorbed and internalized your element. So I can't tell you what to do and how to do it. You need to discover that for yourselves. You are four individuals, each with strong and different personalities and your own way of doing things, but you will need to learn how to work together as one, as a team, so that you can change people's behaviors and lifestyles to secure a healthy earth for future generations. The continuation of your species depends on everyone doing the right thing, every single day. Think about how you are going to make every child a hero ... This is both an enormous responsibility and a great honor, and I know you will make me proud."

"What??" shouted Arielle in alarm. "But I still look like myself right now. Are you not going to change our appearances to make us look more like heroes? Why would anyone believe us?"

"Not cool at all," said Franco, shaking his head in dismay. "Are you just going to give us these powers and then leave us to figure it all out?"

"Also," said Tara, "where do you live? Where do we find you if we have more questions?"

Mizu stood there listening to all of them ask the same questions he had. Since they were more outspoken than him, he remained quiet. He hoped, though, that Mother Nature would answer them—because he wasn't sure he understood exactly what process they were supposed to follow. Or even what they were supposed to do.

Mother Nature smiled. "I understand all of your questions and frustrations. I'll always be here for you, but I don't live in any specific place. You see, the earth is my home, so I live all over. When you need me, you can call on me by combining all of your powers together."

"But what do you mean 'combine our powers together' to call you?" asked Arielle with rising panic in her voice. "Won't it be easier to just text or call you on your cell phone? Or maybe set up some 'face time' on Skype, or we can all create a WhatsApp group like I have with my girlfriends. We're called 'Shopping Girls.' It's fun," she added excitedly. "Wouldn't that be easier than counting on us all to be in the same place at the same time? What if I need you and I can't find the rest of the group?"

Birdie could not hold herself back any longer. "Arielle," she said, "maybe you should invite Mother Nature to join you and your friends at the mall."

"What a great idea," said Arielle excitedly—until she realized Birdie was messing with her. She crossed her arms and said sarcastically, "Really funny, Birdie!"

"You realize you're talking to Mother Nature, right?" asked Birdie as she enjoyed a good laugh at Arielle's expense.

"Birdie, don't be so hard on her," said Mother Nature, realizing the dynamic between these two would be particularly interesting. She looked at Arielle and smiled. "No, my dear, I don't use a cell phone or any other modern technology."

Tara watched Birdie laughing and could not keep the smile off her face. Stifling her laugh, she glanced over at Arielle and thought to herself with a giggle, *This girl really is clueless if she thinks Mother Nature uses a cell phone.*

Mizu was also confused and trying to understand what Mother Nature meant, so he repeated Arielle's question in the hopes of getting a clear set of instructions. "So, umm, how do we do that, combine our powers?"

"Mizu," said Mother Nature with a grin, "I am sure you guys will find a way if you just think about it. You all have your different talents; this is the time to use them."

The four heroes stood there staring at Mother Nature's smiling face, totally confused and overwhelmed. *This has to be some kind of dream,* they all thought, and they were all going to wake up soon.

Things like this just didn't happen in real life.

Mother Nature interrupted their thoughts and said, "I know I've given you a lot to think about and you need some time to process it all." She walked out of the middle of the circle and turned to the group. "Don't forget you are now four, with one mission—to save the earth. But to do that, you must learn how to work together as one. Goodbye for now."

Arielle could not help herself and shouted, "Wait, Mother Nature, let's take a selfie before you go. Nobody will ever believe this!"

Mother Nature winked at Arielle and smiled wisely. "Nice try, Arielle, but I don't appear in photos. Only the four of you can see and hear me. I have made myself known to you only because of our mission."

"After everything you have just been told, only you would have selfies with Mother Nature at the top of your priorities," Birdie said in a huff, and flew from Arielle's shoulder to test out her new wings some more.

"Well, it's not every day that I get to meet Mother Nature, silly," Arielle proclaimed with her hands on her hips. "And a selfie with her would be way awesome!" #PicOfTheYear!"

"It's not every day that your favorite toy comes to life, either," said Birdie as she circled overhead, laughing.

Mother Nature interrupted Arielle and Birdie, knowing their banter could get out of hand quickly. She needed to return to tell Earth the great news. "My heroes, I have given you a lot to think about and now I must go. Call on me whenever you feel the need. I am always here for you."

She spun around once, her long white skirt billowing out around her, and floated upward.

The four kids waved goodbye as she soared up into the clouds. Standing shoulder to shoulder, they looked up at the sky, once complete strangers and now bonded by a common destiny.

Franco broke the silence. "Wow, guys! This is something else. It started out all awkward, but now we're a team, bonded to each other through the spirits of the four elements. This feels so unreal...like a dream."

"Yeah, you're right," Tara agreed, then added quietly to herself, "I guess someone heard my wish and made my dream come true."

Franco overheard her. "Which wish are you talking about?"

"Oh, nothing. I was just thinking out loud," answered Tara quickly. She didn't want to share her innermost thoughts with kids she had just met. She didn't want them to think she was weird, like everyone else did. After all, she was going to be spending a lot of time with them.

"I need to adjust to the idea of Birdie talking now," Arielle said to her new friends. "And having an opinion!"

"Yeah, this has got to be special. I would love to know more about Birdie from when she was just a toy. How long have you been carrying her with you?" Franco asked, thinking this was a good opportunity to get to know her.

Arielle was so embarrassed she wished she had the power to disappear. However, she knew that even if she avoided the question now, it would come up again at some point. She looked over at Tara and Mizu, who both looked like they wanted to hear the story, and twisted her hair around her finger as she slowly started to answer. "So, umm..." she began.

Birdie flew down and jumped in to answer. "You're taking too long, Arielle. I'll tell the story. It started when Arielle's parents..."

Before Birdie could say another word, Arielle snatched her out of the air, pinching her beak closed between her thumb and forefinger.

Birdie mumbled and tried to speak, but nothing could come out through Arielle's vice-like grip.

Arielle giggled at having got one over on her sassy companion, then faced the other three and said, "Maybe we should all go away and think about everything. It's been a long day and Birdie and I are tired." She looked pointedly at Birdie and added, "Aren't we, Birdie?"

Birdie gave another muffled sound. She knew she was beaten. She shrugged her wings and nodded.

"Let's meet back here on Monday after school to form our plan," Arielle suggested, holding Birdie's beak closed, just in case.

"Good idea," agreed Tara. "I need time to get my head around all of this."

"Okay then," said Mizu. "I also need some time to think about what we're going to do. Mother Nature left us with a lot to figure out."

"Right," said Franco, taking the lead. "It's getting late, so let's at least exchange numbers so we can get in touch with each other if we need to."

After trading phone numbers, they waved to one another as they all headed home.

Chapter 6

# Reality Sinks In

Sunday went by with the new heroes in a daze, as they tried to process and accept what they'd been told.

Feeling confused, Arielle sat on her bed. This whole hero thing still seemed like a bizarre dream, especially with Birdie flying around the room and talking nonstop.

"If you keep on frowning like that, you're going to get some major wrinkles," Birdie said, perched on the windowsill.

Arielle looked up, irritated. "You're supposed to be helping me," she said accusingly.

"Hey, I'm just trying to lighten the mood. Stop acting like this is a disaster, when it's actually the beginning of a new and exciting adventure in which *you* get to play a big part. It's not like you went to school and discovered someone else wearing the same outfit! Now *that* would be the end of the world!" Birdie chuckled. She absolutely *loved* being able to talk now, and messing with Arielle was super fun.

"Well if we don't get this mission right, it may well be the end of the world," Arielle said seriously. "I still feel like this is some sort of dream — all of these powers…a team of four…how is this going to work? We are four very different kids. And how will we look? I mean, will everyone know I have powers? I don't look any different, but this power is in me forever, I guess…Or at least until we complete our mission. I'm so confused right now, and the weirdest part is being able to talk to you about all of this." She sighed dramatically.

"What on earth is wrong with you?" Birdie asked. "So I'm real now—deal with it! I'm here and we have a lot to do together. You always used to wish you could talk to me, but instead of being happy, your head has been totally up in the clouds since yesterday. You should be excited because *you* get to save the world. You know, you'll probably be famous! I can see it now: Ladies and gentlemen, let's give a round of applause for the one and only planet hero, Arielle." Birdie delivered the last line a bit sarcastically. She knew how much Arielle loved attention and how she longed to do something to make herself famous.

While Birdie was clearly making fun of her, Arielle couldn't help but imagine herself on stage, wearing an amazing designer outfit and waving to the applauding crowd as she accepted the Nobel Peace Prize for saving the planet. Her Instagram takeover would be legendary!

Birdie watched her waving to herself and interrupted irritably, "Arielle, are you listening to me?"

Arielle shook her head. "Yeah, I guess you're right," she said, totally missing the sarcasm. "It's just so much to process, you know, and a whole lot of responsibility. Yesterday I was just a cute, popular, and amazingly talented cheerleader, and now I'm a superhero who has to fly around making sure people respect the earth." She waved her arms around as she spoke—a sure sign of how unsettled she felt.

"You forgot modest," Birdie added with even more sarcasm in her voice. "You have only said the same thing like a hundred times since we left the park." Birdie flew over to sit on Arielle's shoulder and give her ear a nip, and added, "You have to snap out of it. It is what it is!"

Arielle sighed again.

Birdie decided some distraction was in order, because she just couldn't handle Arielle being so gloomy. "Oh my gosh!" she shrieked. "How can you be seen like this? Just *look* at those nails of yours!"

Arielle looked down at the chipped nail polish on her fingers and jumped up in shock. "#MakeOverASAP!" she said. "Time for a manicure!"

Arielle got out all her nail stuff and sat down at her desk. After removing the polish, she looked over at Birdie and said, "Thanks. This is just what I needed to take my mind off things. You're a great friend—as always."

"We're in this together, Arielle, and I'll always be here for you. I'm glad you're starting to feel a bit better about things now."

Arielle looked at Birdie seriously and said, "#GetMyActTogether. I can't let myself go like this again. If I'm going to be famous, I need to keep on top of my personal grooming. Chipped nails—I can't believe I've been walking around like this!"

"Don't worry," Birdie said with a raised eyebrow. "Your secret is safe. I won't call the fashion police."

"Ha ha, very funny."

Birdie squawked excitedly. "That's it! You know how you said earlier that you wondered how you would look and if people would recognize you?"

"Yeah," Arielle replied, distracted with filing her nails. "What's your point?"

"My point," said Birdie, hopping over and plucking the nail file out of Arielle's hands so she could focus, "is that you have great fashion sense. You should think about designing a really cute outfit to wear when you activate your powers."

Arielle looked doubtfully at Birdie. Before she could protest, Birdie continued, "You're good at stuff like this! Just promise that you'll at least think about it."

Then, just as Arielle opened her mouth to speak, Birdie ruffled her feathers and hopped onto the ledge by the open window. "I'm going out now to stretch my wings for a bit. Just think about what I said and we can talk about it more when I get back, okay?"

She ruffled her feathers again, and before Arielle could stop her, flew out the window.

Arielle opened a bottle of polish and began painting her nails absentmindedly. She stared out the window in a bit of a daze, watching Birdie fly off into the distance and thinking to herself, *Designing my own costume for my special powers will be fun. And if I'm going to be saving the world, I may as well look good doing it! I'll need to talk to the others about it, too."*

The more she thought about it, the more she liked the idea. She was so caught up in her fashion daydream that when she looked down at her nails again she let out a shriek. Instead of her usual sparkly polish, she had unknowingly picked up a bottle of White Out and painted her nails with it.

"ARRGH!" she shouted. "I have to get a grip!"

● ● ● ●

Across town, Tara wasn't having a much better time. As soon as she woke up, she climbed her tree to think. She needed to relax and process all that had happened yesterday. Settling down on her favorite branch to meditate, she said to herself, "We're four special kids who Mother Nature chose for this mission, and I'm excited to be part of this team to save the earth."

She knew she sounded completely crazy, sitting up in a tree talking to herself, but she always found it easier to process things when she spoke out loud and could hear her thoughts. So she kept going.

"And before she left, Mother Nature said we need to work together as one. Hmm." She paused. One way to come together as a team would be to have a special name—something that united them and fit with the mission. "I'll need to discuss this with the others and see what they think."

She was so excited about this idea that she nearly fell out of the tree. As she gripped a branch, hanging on for dear life and trying to catch her breath, she could have sworn she heard two squirrels talking about her.

"Tara is not herself today," said one.

"Mother Nature, team, mission… What is she talking about? Maybe we should move closer to her and find out if she's okay," said the other.

Tara shook her head. She was *definitely* going crazy. There was no other explanation for being able to hear squirrels talking.

*Unless…* said the small, nagging voice in the back of her head that she hadn't been able to shake since noon the previous day. *Unless what Mother Nature told you is the truth.*

She needed more time to think this all through, so she did what she usually did when she struggled with something and needed to burn off restless energy. She climbed down from the tree, gathered her things, and headed to the beach to pick up trash.

*I think it will be much safer if I keep my feet on the ground today,* she thought.

● ● ● ●

Needing to feel the water around him so he could think, Mizu had gone surfing. Despite the flat ocean, he had been out in the water since dawn. Now the sun was high in the sky. He had hesitated and debated with himself all day, knowing he had to get home soon but still toying with the same idea.

He was still in disbelief about yesterday's encounter with Mother Nature. And if it really was possible for him to control water, this new ability would challenge everything he knew and respected as a young scientist. He wasn't sure he was ready to let that go just yet. For as long as he could remember, every question he'd ever had could be answered by science. This new reality most definitely defied every scientific principle he had ever been taught. If it was indeed his destiny, he would have to change most of his views about the world he lived in.

He waded out of the ocean, shook the water off, and sat down on the warm sand. As he stared out at the horizon, mulling over all that happened yesterday, he thought to himself, *We might have all these cool powers, but it still feels like something is missing. We need something to connect us to our power — something that makes us different from our regular selves. The last thing I need is for the kids at school to recognize me and have another reason to tease and laugh at me.*

As he continued gazing out at the horizon, suddenly a brilliant idea struck him. A huge smile spread across his face.

*I don't know why I didn't think of this before!* he thought. *I need to let the others know I think I can invent something—something that will allow us to transform when we connect with our powers so we look different. If this works, we can be anonymous and still save the earth.*

He laughed out loud at his idea and thought, *Hmm, I think Tara and Franco would like to be anonymous and not recognized by their friends or others. I'm not so sure about Arielle though.*

He decided that since the sea was especially calm, he might as well head home and work on developing his idea. As he gathered up his things, though, he noticed a group of surfers bemoaning the lack of waves. Mizu recognized them from school, but as usual they didn't seem to know who he was.

"Dude, this blows," said one.

"Totally!" agreed the second.

"Nothing worse than a flat sea," complained the third.

"Let's go home, then," said the fourth as he started to gather up his belongings.

Mizu wished he could go up to them and chat, because as a surfer he completely understood how they felt. There was *nothing* on earth worse than needing to surf but having to sit on the sand instead and watch a calm sea stretch out in front of you for miles.

He sat for a minute and thought about how he could make things better, running his hands through his wet hair and sighing as he went over the argument for the thousandth time in the last few hours.

*Right, that's it,* he thought. *I have to know! If there was ever a day to test out my new power, today is it!*

He sat down at the water's edge and took a good look around to make sure no one was paying attention to him. When he was sure he wouldn't be noticed, Mizu tapped his feet in the water with the hope of seeing another great wave appear. He tapped and waited. Nothing. He tapped again and waited a bit longer, willing the ocean to rise up in front of him. Then he squeezed his eyes shut and concentrated as hard as he could on imagining a great wave curling toward the shore. He opened his eyes again…and again, nothing had happened.

*Okay, one last try,* he thought.

This time, he saw himself riding a wave. He imagined how the wind would feel rushing past him as he sped along toward the shore, and how the cool water would splash down around his body as the wave rolled around him. He heard the roaring sound that he loved more than anything, as it meant the waves were good.

His eyes were still closed when he heard one of the surfers shout, "Whoa, check out that ginormous wave! Let's go!"

Another one yelled, "Where did that come from? Let's get out there!"

Mizu quickly opened his eyes and saw the huge wave he had just created. He paused for a moment, smiled broadly, and said aloud, "Awesome! So it *does* work!"

Not wanting to be left behind, he jumped up, grabbed his board, and ran into the water with all the other surfers to ride the wave. A few seconds later he felt the board lift from under him as he caught the wave, and laughed out loud as he rode what he'd created back to shore.

Mizu landed in the shallow surf, still laughing, and wiped the water out of his eyes. He looked around and saw quite a few happy surfers and just as many puzzled beachgoers wondering where that huge wave came from. There was still some time before he had to get home, so he commanded the sea to give them a few more good rides. *What good is the power to control water if I don't use it?* he thought, feeling happier than he had in days. As he was getting ready to leave the beach, he paused to look back out to the horizon. The sea was once again flat as a board.

"Dude," said one of the other surfers as they walked past Mizu, who was gathering up his things. "That was super lucky. There have been no waves all day!"

"Yeah," Mizu agreed. "*Super* lucky!"

He grinned the whole way home.

It was Sunday and Franco was home alone—again. His dad was running a weekend seminar and his mom had been asked to go into work to train a new staff member. Meanwhile, Franco, who usually hung out with his buddies when his parents were working and therefore rarely by himself, was actually happy to have some "alone" time to process what had happened. He was still feeling pretty confused about it all. He unwrapped another piece of gum and popped it in his mouth. As he chewed, his mind wandered to the meeting the previous day.

*Maybe it was just a dream,* he thought. *I'm probably just obsessing over that cheerleader because I didn't get to talk to her at the game, so now my brain is playing tricks on me.*

But even as he tried to rationalize what had happened, a part of him knew there was no logical explanation. Deep down, he knew it hadn't been a dream. He just didn't know what to do with the information he had been given. Franco was not big on thinking things through—he was more of a doer—but what could he possibly do? He didn't want to contact the other kids and seem like the only one who was a little freaked out by all this, but time was dragging and it felt like Monday would never arrive. He had never been a very patient person, and the waiting was making him restless.

"Ok, so what now?" he asked himself out loud. He felt like he needed to be doing something useful and not just sitting around thinking about the same things over and over. Then he thought, *Mother Nature said we need to come together as a team, but then gave us each different powers from the four elements—earth, air, fire and water. We should have something that highlights our elements to show where our powers come from.*

"ARRGH! I have such a headache," he moaned. "I hate all this thinking!" He rolled over to the edge of his bed, needing to forget about this whole thing for a while and lose himself in some fantasy. He opened his new comic book and tried to engross himself in the story, but something he couldn't quite put his finger on was niggling in the back of his brain. He tossed the comic across the room in frustration. It fell open on the floor near his window.

"That was dumb," he said to himself. "Reading comics isn't going to help." He got up to pick it up and put it away, but when he saw the page it had opened to, something in his brain kicked into gear. It was a double-page spread advertising a comic book convention that had happened a few months back. All the major comic book heroes were on the page, and as Franco stared at it, he got inspired.

"That's it!" he shouted. "We all need our own special symbols, like Superman, Batman, and Wonder Woman have! I'll bring it up when I see the others tomorrow and see what they think. It will be fun to draw them for everyone."

He smiled to himself as he thought about different ideas he could pitch to the others for their symbols. "This is going to be so cool!"

Franco reached under his bed and pulled out his skateboard to clean and oil the wheels. He felt like he needed to keep himself busy until he met up with the group again. As he grabbed the end of his skateboard, he realized the house was deathly quiet. He wasn't used to being alone and he needed as much distraction as possible, so he looked through his music collection.

Franco loved listening to all kinds of music — equal parts pop, rock, and modern Latino. It always seemed to calm him down when he was stressed or anxious, and after the meeting with Mother Nature he was more stressed and anxious than he had ever been.

On the one hand, he was now kind of a hero, and that was beyond awesome, but he had never really thought about the responsibility that went along with being a hero. He had always thought it was just action, fun, and winning, but now that he was tasked with saving the earth, he realized there was more to it than simply swooping in and saving the day at the last minute.

He flipped through his dad's record collection and pulled out his favorite Doors album. He carefully removed the vinyl and placed it on top of his turntable, then set the needle over his favorite track—"Light My Fire"—and settled down on the floor to clean and oil his skateboard wheels.

As the music filled the room, he started to relax. He stopped cleaning the wheels for a moment, closed his eyes, and tapped his foot to the beat during the chorus. He loved letting the music wash over him and getting lost in the lyrics. As he chewed on his gum, he snapped his fingers in time to the music. Opening his eyes, he moved his whole body to the rhythm of the song.

As he stared absentmindedly out the window, swaying his body to the song's last chorus, he noticed a movement out of the corner of his eye that also seemed to be in tempo with the beat. When he looked more closely, he was shocked. Every time he snapped his fingers, sparks shot out!

"*Ay caramba!*" he said loudly.

His heart was thumping in his chest and he took big, gulping breaths. He had to be imagining things, surely!

As his breathing slowed down, he started to snap his fingers in time to the beat again, gently at first...and then with more and more force. He watched in amazement as it happened again and again. When he snapped gently, showers of bright red, orange, and yellow sparks flew out of his fingers. When he snapped them harder, a fully formed flame erupted. He was making fire!

"Way cool!" he thought with a grin, and flopped back down onto his bed.

● ● ● ●

As bedtime drew near, the four new heroes settled down for the night, still thinking about all that had happened—how Mother Nature had told them about who they were and their purposes on the earth, and most of all how they had discovered they had special powers. All of them felt excited for Monday when they could share their ideas with each other. The new heroes lay in their own beds, in their own houses, miles apart but joined by an invisible thread that connected them in a way none of them fully understood yet.

Lying in bed, Arielle stared at the outfit she had picked out for the following day, and asked Birdie, "Have you seen my pink sweater?"

When Birdie didn't answer, she looked over to the corner of the room where Birdie had been perched to find her fast asleep on the pink sweater.

"I guess it's comfortable," she said to herself.

Arielle thought she needed peace and quiet from Birdie's comments all day, but as she lay there alone, she really wished Birdie was awake. She was the only one that Arielle could confide in about all of this—the only one who could understand what Arielle was going through.

Arielle smiled. "This is all really happening, isn't it?" she said in a whisper. "I don't know what to feel. Is this all for real? I guess I am really a hero now. The earth is a part of me, and I have a huge responsibility. I hope I have what it takes to make things right."

● ● ● ●

Franco slid under the covers and settled back against his pillows with his hands behind his head. As he stared at the poster of a bright red sports car soaring through a ring of fire, he suddenly became fully aware of what lay ahead. *This is it,* he thought with determination. *I'm not a kid anymore. There is a part of me connected to the earth. I can feel it burning in my heart. I commit to doing my part. Now I know I am a hero, here today to save tomorrow, and I know I can do it.*

● ● ● ●

Tara wiggled around under the covers, trying to get comfortable in the little bit of space left for her. Remus, Freddy, and Chester had already found their spots on her bed and she'd arranged herself around them, trying hard not to wake them up. Her four dogs were already asleep on the floor, so she was the only one who couldn't seem to get settled enough to sleep. As she put her arm gently around a purring Remus, she realized the huge task that lay ahead of her.

"This feeling is so new and now my dream has come true. The earth needs me and I know what I must do," she whispered.

● ● ● ●

Mizu shut down his computer and got into bed. He lay staring at his aquarium full of beautiful fish, finding it soothing to watch the fish swim around and wishing he could live in the water like that. Watching his favorite fish as it blew bubbles, he said, "I must protect my home, and now I'm not alone. I'm part of a team. I've been given something very special and powerful, and I need to use it wisely. I'm not the school nerd anymore. I'm a hero now."

He smiled as he said the words, knowing he had found his place in the world at last.

   As each of them started to realize who they were about to become and the enormous responsibility given to them, they felt a sense of peace. They all fell asleep with smiles

on their faces. They could only dream about the huge adventures that lay ahead of them.

## Reality Sinks In

Chapter 7

# Connecting the Dots

It seemed an eternity for Monday to come around, and even longer to get through the school day. But eventually, 3:00 rolled around and the four new heroes, along with Birdie, met as agreed at the totem pole. They were so eager to share their new ideas that they all started to talk at once. Birdie quickly stepped in to mediate.

"All right, you guys need to take turns if we are going to hear all your ideas. Mizu, you first."

"Me?" said Mizu, surprised that Birdie chose him to go first. People never asked his opinion … or even paid that much attention to him. "I can wait, Birdie."

"Hey!" interrupted Arielle, a bit annoyed. "What kind of loyalty is that to your best friend?"

Birdie winked. "It's not about loyalty. I already know your idea. I'm curious to hear what the others have to say."

"Humph!" said Arielle with a pout as she created a "W" with her thumbs and index fingers. "#Whatever!"

Birdie flew up behind Mizu, flapping her wings as if to usher him forward. Mizu glanced over at Arielle because he didn't want to start off on the wrong foot with his new friends. He was determined that this arrangement would be more than just a mission. He so wanted real friends and knew this was his best shot.

Arielle sighed and shrugged. "Go ahead, Mizu. Let's hear your idea."

Mizu cleared his throat nervously and ran a hand through his dark hair. "Well, I thought about what Mother Nature said about us having to become one, like a team, and have an idea of what we can do to unite us."

"Tell us," Tara said.

"I'm not sure if you guys know, but I'm kind of a science geek," Mizu told them as an embarrassed flush spread up his cheeks.

"#Duh! Tell us something new," Arielle muttered under her breath.

Tara shot her such a fierce look that Arielle quickly clamped her mouth shut and listened. *Why is Curly always on my case? I can't even mutter my own thoughts to myself without her shooting me scary looks,* Arielle thought as she tried to force herself to listen to Mizu.

Mizu didn't hear Arielle's comment, and kept talking as if she hadn't said anything—which peeved her even more.

"I like to tinker around with gadgets and take them apart and see how they work. Sometimes I use the parts from different things to make new gadgets. I guess you could say I'm sort of an inventor."

Franco looked intrigued. "Go on," he urged.

"Well, I think I can invent some kind of device to connect us to our powers. It would also help protect our identities. I don't know about you guys, but I know if I went to school and told everyone I was a hero, I'd be a laughingstock. Well, even more of a laughingstock than I already am," he added quietly. "And no one would take me seriously."

"I was just thinking that none of us really knows what we're doing here, and I'm sure a lot of this is going to be trial and error until we get it right. I'd just prefer not to be making mistakes for all the world to see. Besides, I'm not popular like you two," he said, gesturing to Arielle and Franco. "I'll have a really hard time getting people to listen to me as myself."

He hung his head, clearly embarrassed at having revealed his nerd status to his new friends.

"I think that's brilliant, Mizu," Franco said.

"Very clever," Tara agreed

"You totally read my mind, Mizu," Arielle said with a smile. "My idea kind of fits in with yours."

"Really?" Mizu asked, relieved he hadn't been laughed at or teased for his idea.

"Yeah, I wasn't too excited about the idea of running around telling people I'm a hero now, either," Arielle said seriously. "I could lose all my Instagram followers who look at me for fashion advice, and that would be a total disaster."

Birdie snorted. "The survival of the planet is at stake and you're worried about how many Instagram followers you have? Arielle, I love you, but your priorities are really out of whack."

"It took me a few years to build my reputation at school as a fashion expert, as well as my number of followers, so I don't want to take the risk and become, like, the joke of the year," said Arielle with a squinty-eyed smile. "So I totally agree with Mizu's idea of being anonymous when we change into our hero selves. And if you look at all the heroes from history, they kept their hero status separate from their private lives. Plus, they had unique outfits that looked great. And studies have shown that people are far more likely to listen to pretty people who are dressed nicely than someone plain and ordinary. And yes, that's a real fact and not just my opinion."

"That totally sounds like something she would say," Tara whispered to Birdie.

"If we look cool, I think people will pay more attention to our message," Arielle continued to explain her point. "Better than if we approach them looking the way we do now." She looked pointedly at Tara, who just rolled her eyes.

"You make a good point, Arielle," said Franco. He knew girly girls like her were not always taken seriously when they tried to talk about serious subjects—especially by studious kids like Tara and Mizu. But he thought she was right, and wanted to show her so.

While Tara didn't like it and would rather die than admit that Arielle was right, she had experienced first-hand that people didn't seem to respond to her when she tried to recruit volunteers to pick up trash or help with a conservation project. She might think the cheerleader was a total airhead, but this time she had a point. Although she agreed with Arielle, that didn't stop her from being annoyed with the way she kept going on about her Instagram followers and popularity. She thought that part was dumb, but she held her tongue for the sake of peace.

"Okay, so what do you propose then, Arielle?" she asked.

"I was thinking I could design each of us a special outfit to wear when we activate our powers. Something that makes us stand out and look like real heroes. We might have a serious mission to fulfill, but that doesn't mean we can't look good in the process."

"I think that's a great idea," Franco said.

"You would agree with her if she suggested that we start eating snails," Tara said pointedly.

Franco glared back at her, but couldn't argue. He definitely had a soft spot for Arielle's pretty face, and had not yet given up trying to impress her. So he jumped in with his idea, hoping the team would like it while taking the spotlight off his Arielle crush.

"After I realized that we're real heroes now," he said, "I was on my bed flipping through my comic books and noticed that each hero has a symbol that represents them and their power. So I thought we should each have our own symbol for our powers too, you know, like Batman, Superman, and all the rest. And once I've drawn them, you can put them onto our outfits." He looked at Arielle and smiled hopefully.

"That's a great idea," Arielle said. "I can't wait to have my own symbol and a whole new look."

"Mizu, you're too quiet over there. What do you think about my idea?" asked Franco.

"Oh, sorry Franco," said Mizu, who was still getting used to sharing his opinions. "Yes, I think that's a clever idea."

Franco was glad they all liked his idea and could not wait to start working on the sketches.

Now it was Tara's turn to share her big idea. Everyone turned to her.

"I think your ideas are all really good," Tara began. "I was thinking the other day, like you Franco, about the whole hero thing. And I came up with the idea to have a team name that will represent who we are. You know, something like X-Men or The Avengers or Justice League, but more related to our mission. That way everyone we meet will know us by that name. It will join us all together as a team, just like Mother Nature said."

Franco was the first to respond. "Wow, such a great idea, Tara."

*Now why didn't I think of that?* he thought to himself.

"Tara, I really like your idea. We should definitely have a name," Mizu added as he started to feel more comfortable speaking up with his new friends.

Tara was happy to get such a positive response from the guys, but Arielle clearly didn't seem in a hurry to share her feelings.

Birdie was sitting on Arielle's shoulder and thought she was being mean by keeping quiet about Tara's idea. She held herself back from biting Arielle's ear to reprimand her for being unkind, and instead whispered, "Arielle, you should say something nice to Tara."

"Oh, all right! I'm still thinking about it," Arielle replied in a snappy whisper. Birdie knew Arielle's competitive spirit well, and knew it was hard for her to admit that Tara also had a good idea. She noticed Tara looking over at Arielle for any comments, and decided to break the tension.

"So, Tara, did you come up with any possible names?" she asked.

Tara could tell that Arielle was reluctant to say anything, so she thought of a way to get her attention. She answered Birdie as seriously as she could while trying to conceal her smile. "Sure. One is 'Team Selfie.'"

Franco and Mizu smiled at each other. They knew Tara was messing with Arielle. But they held back their laughter because they didn't want Arielle to think they were laughing at her.

Birdie glanced over at Arielle, thinking she would be agitated by Tara's joke at her expense. They all held their breath when Arielle started to speak.

"Who would've thought that you knew how to be silly and make jokes? I didn't think you had a sense of humor—you seem so serious all the time. I'm starting to see there's another side to you that I didn't think you had. That was pretty funny," she said with a wink.

They all breathed a sigh of relief. Tensions were running high already, and the last thing they needed was for two of the four team members to be at each other's throats all the time.

"I have to admit," Arielle said after they all had a good giggle, "I like your idea of having a name for our team, but try to think about something cool for us. The selfie thing is mine."

Then Franco stepped up and said, "We've all come up with some awesome ideas but it sounds like we still have some work to do. I say we go home and get started on all this and meet back here next

Monday, to see what we've come up with."

They all agreed in a chorus of "Okay!"

After exchanging goodbyes, they parted in different directions as they each headed for home. Birdie said to Arielle, "You were so cool with Tara. I really thought you were going to let her have it over that joke, but you showed a side I've never seen."

Arielle laughed. "Well, I'm still liking my manicure from yesterday and didn't want to break a nail by scratching out her eyes."

With that, Birdie gave her friend a playful wink as the two continued towards home.

Chapter 8

# Four Become One

During the following week, Mizu could not stop thinking about the gadget he needed to invent for his team. He was so consumed by his new project that for the first time ever he didn't pay attention in class. He didn't even notice when Mr. Reichman asked him a question about the experiment they were supposed to be doing.

When Mizu didn't respond, Mr. Reichman asked, "Mizu, are you okay?"

Mizu was so caught up in his thoughts that he just shook his head. It looked as if he was saying no, he wasn't all right, but in actuality he was mentally eliminating ideas for his gadget.

Mr. Reichman, not used to his star pupil being anything less than stellar, asked in a concerned tone, "No? What's wrong?"

When Mizu didn't look up, Mr. Reichman said "Mizu?" very loudly, and this snapped Mizu back to the present. "What's the matter? You shook your head when I asked if you were okay."

Mizu was embarrassed. He had been so lost in thought that he hadn't realized Mr. Reichman was addressing him. "Umm, sorry sir," he stammered. "Not...no... I didn't mean to say no... I mean, I'm fine..." He trailed off as he looked around the classroom and noticed everyone laughing at him.

"He is totally spaced out," said one of the cool guys from the back of the room, and then the rest of the class laughed even harder.

"What a loser," said another.

"No wonder he has no friends," said someone else.

"Okay, kids, that's enough," commanded Mr. Reichman. "Let's get back to work."

The laughter died down as Mizu slid down in his seat, feeling mortified.

"And Mizu," Mr. Reichman added. "If you aren't feeling well, go see the school nurse. You haven't been yourself today."

A very embarrassed Mizu quietly responded, "No, that's okay, sir. It won't happen again." He tried very hard to concentrate for the rest of the lesson.

• • • •

When Saturday finally arrived, Mizu was excited to have the weekend to work uninterrupted on his idea. He had a very particular process when he set about inventing something. He liked to start with a sketch to get a feel for how the finished piece would look. But this was the first time he didn't have any ideas for how it should look.

He sat at his desk with a clean sheet of paper in front of him, waiting for inspiration and chewing anxiously on the end of his pencil, hoping for an Aha! moment. But so far his brain had been most uncooperative. He was starting to feel very stressed. Maybe he had overstated his abilities to the other three. Maybe he couldn't do this. He hadn't wanted to be the only one without an idea, but maybe this was a tad too ambitious, even for the science guy.

*You have to pull yourself together, Mizu,* he chided himself. *You can't be the weak link that lets the team down. THINK, THINK!*

After a few minutes, he began to sketch a helmet gadget that had wires coming out of it—wires that would activate their powers when they put the helmet on. He finished the sketch and examined the end result critically, then scrunched up the paper and tossed it into the trashcan. A helmet would be too heavy and bulky to carry around with them. It would also have people asking questions, since they were still all too young to ride motorcycles.

*I can just imagine Arielle's reaction to wearing a helmet. She would throw a fit because it would mess up her hair!*

He grabbed another sheet and tried to think of something cool and stylish. But since he wasn't cool or stylish he struggled to come up with ideas. He thought maybe a belt or shoes, but quickly dismissed those as they might clash with what Arielle was designing. Then he sketched another idea—special sunglasses that looked normal so nobody could tell that they were actually devices used for activating the heroes' powers.

*No, no, no, these won't work either because if we wear them when it's not bright and sunny, people will think we're crazy.*

Getting frustrated with himself, he scribbled over his drawing and cried, "None of this is going to work! I can't think of anything."

Then he pushed everything on his desk onto the floor and said, "Everyone is going to think I'm a fool after promising to come up with something. I've only got two days left. I'm running out of time."

He threw himself down on his bed in despair. He needed an idea and fast. After a moment, he sat up and leaned against the wall, staring out of his open window and waiting for something to come to him.

*I just need to relax. I'm too on edge to think straight,* he thought as he looked around his room. "Oh, wow! My room is a mess. I need to get this cleaned up before my mom sees it," he said to himself as he climbed off the bed to pick up the clothes and trash littering the room.

While he was cleaning up the mess he had made, he noticed that he had tossed his fancy new diving watch onto the floor during his tantrum. "Phew! Good thing it didn't break. I need to be more careful with this," he muttered to himself. "If I break this watch, my parents will be super mad—"

And that's when the idea hit him. He laughed out loud at himself for not thinking of it before. *It's literally been staring me in the face all week,* he thought, shaking his head.

He hurried over to his desk and frantically sketched his new idea, getting more and more excited as he watched it come to life on the paper.

When Sunday morning dawned, Mizu stretched and yawned loudly. He hadn't slept a wink because he was up all night, totally absorbed in working on his invention. He was so proud of himself for having nearly completed the four cool digital watches. Everything had come together seamlessly from his sketches, and all that remained was developing an app for each one—something to use when they wanted to activate their powers. He also wanted to add their outfits into the apps, but needed to speak to Arielle first because he needed her fashion skills for this part.

He collapsed onto his bed, excited to show the group the sketches he created. Feeling happy and satisfied, he fell into a deep and peaceful sleep.

• • • •

Arielle decided to hit the mall to get inspiration for their new hero costumes. But while shopping usually made her feel better, today she felt rather glum as she trawled through the shops, examining all the latest fashions with a critical eye. This was the first time she had ever been shopping without her closest friends Sarah, Kalpana, Nancy, and Angelica. She felt even worse because she had received a few text messages from them that morning on her WhatsApp group, "Shopping Girls," and hadn't responded. After everything that had happened, she didn't think she could pretend she was just a regular girl hanging out with her friends at the mall—and confiding in them was out of the question. She knew if she told them about her hero powers, they would think she was crazy.

*I wish Birdie was here to help me out,* she thought. But that wasn't going to happen. Now that she was a real bird, she did what she pleased rather than staying with Arielle all the time. Besides, having a real live bird flying around the mall was sure to attract unwanted attention.

Arielle laughed to herself at the irony of the situation. While a few weeks ago she would have done anything to be the center of attention, now she wasn't so sure that drawing attention to herself was a good idea. At least not until they had this whole "hero team" thing figured out.

She had looked in lots of shops but hadn't found any inspiration for their outfits, and worse still, she hadn't found anything she was tempted to buy for herself. This was the first time she could ever remember leaving the mall empty-handed.

*Oh well, I guess I had better go home, then. I'll have to look in my fashion magazines and online for some ideas for these outfits. There's bound to be something that inspires me.*

Arielle was on the escalator, heading down toward the exit of the mall, when suddenly her heart leapt up into her throat. Sarah, Kalpana, Nancy, and Angelica had just entered and were heading straight toward her. Starting to panic, she turned around and tried running back up the escalator. After a minute or so, she was too exhausted to continue. She regained her poise and tried to project confidence as she descended toward them. Meanwhile, she was frantically wracking her brain to explain why she had ignored their texts and come alone. Fortunately they hadn't spotted her yet, as she was still on the escalator and the mall was packed.

*Maybe I'll be able to sneak past them when I get down,* she thought. *#SoAwkward! This hero thing is totally going to mess up my social life!*

She noticed that her friends were each wearing a beautifully colored dress. Sarah had on a cute, puffy purple one that really suited her. Kalpana's was a pretty dark green, and Nancy wore a bright, fire-engine red one that really complemented her figure. And Angelica's soft turquoise dress reminded her of the seaside. She quietly said to herself, "That's it! Those are the colors I'll use for our outfits."

Completely lost in her thoughts and excitement, Arielle hadn't realized she was at the bottom of the escalator. She stumbled and bumped into a little boy with an ice cream cone, knocking it out of his hand. The ice cream catapulted forward and landed—*splat!*—on the floor. Almost immediately, the little boy began to howl and scream—an ear-splitting, deafeningly loud wail that made everyone stop dead in their tracks.

Arielle tried to placate the boy, but he just ran off to his mother, who was sitting nearby. He threw himself dramatically down onto the floor, with his little fists hitting the ground as he writhed around throwing the hugest tantrum Arielle had ever seen. The commotion drew looks from almost everybody in the food court and Arielle, feeling mortified, tried to make a hasty escape. As she stepped carefully over the mess of spilt ice cream, trying not to get any on her shoes, she heard a familiar voice and froze.

"Arielle!!! What are you doing here?" asked Sarah, casting an annoyed look at her. "I thought we said the five of us would always shop together." The other girls looked confused and upset as well.

Arielle looked at them and didn't really know what to say. They all seemed mad at her, and were clearly waiting for an answer. She lowered her head, looking as if she was going to cry.

Her friends were shocked. Arielle *never* lost her cool. She was always in control of herself, and none of them had ever seen her cry before. In fact, she was always scathing toward others she saw crying, claiming it made their faces all red and blotchy—an unforgivable fashion sin.

"Oh, Arielle, are you okay?" asked Sarah. "I'm sorry I raised my voice, but I was worried about you. We all were. Right, girls?"

She turned to the others and shrugged her shoulders. She had no idea what to do or how to handle this situation.

Arielle was a pretty good actress and knew her friends well, so she turned on the water works. She raised her head, tears streaming down her face, torn between being pleased that she was such a good actress and feeling terrible for purposely deceiving her friends this way. But she had no idea what else to do. Since she never had had such an emotional outburst, she knew it would throw them and buy her some time to think.

"Oh God, it's just terrible," she wailed through heaving sniffles. "My life is, like, totally over." She put her hand to her forehead for added dramatic effect.

Her friends stared at her, expressions of horror on their pretty faces.

Kalpana clutched Nancy's hand, bracing herself for the worst, while Angelica chewed nervously on a fingernail.

"Well, when I was in the bathroom getting ready this morning, I decided to take my morning selfie. The phone slipped and fell into the toilet. #SoGross. I reached in and grabbed it as fast as I could, then tried to dry it off, but it wouldn't turn back on. So I came to the mall to get it fixed but they just told me that it might take a week to repair—if they can fix it at all. My phone might be totally destroyed, and my mom said she wasn't going to replace it as she had just bought me this one. How am I going to live without a phone?"

Arielle let out a great, gasping sob as she delivered the final sentence, and looked at her friends with bucket-loads of tears filling her eyes.

Her friends all had their hands over their mouths in horror. This was awful news, and it explained why Arielle looked so miserable.

"So you see, I couldn't text you guys," she continued. "And what's worse is that I couldn't take my selfies this morning, so my day started all wrong and now I won't be able to take any selfies or update my Instagram account for a whole week!"

She started to cry and sob even more loudly. The girls felt bad for her because they knew they would die if they had to be without their phones.

Sarah hugged Arielle and told her, "I guess you've really had a tough day today, I'm sorry I was so hard on you. Do you want us to stay with you for the rest of the day?"

Arielle wiped her eyes and said, "Thanks, you girls are great, but I don't want to bring you down, too. You guys stay and do your shopping. I'm going to go home and lie down."

"You're still in shock," Sarah agreed. "Some rest will do you good. Just text us on the group chat when you get your phone back, okay?"

"I promise," Arielle said.

They all gave Arielle a hug and, after saying their goodbyes, continued walking toward the escalators.

Arielle smiled to herself in relief, knowing that her friends had bought her act and believed her story. "#BestActingEver!" she said to herself.

When she was sure they were out of sight, she pulled her phone out of her bag and told it, "I don't know what I'd do without you, so don't you even think about breaking up with me!" She kissed it, took a quick selfie, and left the mall, excited to meet up with her new group on Monday to share her ideas for their outfits.

• • • •

It was Sunday, and Franco had been at church all morning. He liked going there because it always filled him with positive energy and inspired him when he needed it. When the service let out, he hopped on his skateboard and sped toward home so he could work on the visual icons for each of the heroes' powers.

When he got close to his house, Franco saw his buddies hanging out on the sidewalk. Even though he was in a hurry to get started with his drawings, he stopped because he didn't want them to think that he was ignoring them.

"*Hola amigos*, what's up?"

"Oh, hey, Franco, we were just talking about you," said Marco. "We haven't seen you around for a few days. Everything good with you?"

"Yes!" Franco replied. "Everything's great. What have you got there?" he added, pointing to the magazine in Marco's hand.

"It's next year's car collection. My dad gave it to me this morning," Marco said, holding it up so Franco could see the cover.

"Oh cool, can I take a look?" asked Franco. "You know how much I love cars, and I haven't seen this one yet."

Marco handed over the magazine and Franco began to flip through the pages. He loved to imagine himself driving the cars he saw in these magazines, and really couldn't wait for the day he got his license. Even though he knew the chances were slim that he would ever drive one of these fancy cars, it didn't hurt to dream, right?

As he turned the pages, a bright red car caught his eye. It was a shiny, sleek, streamlined sports car—a beautiful modern shape, with chrome finishes. It was truly one of the most spectacular cars Franco had ever seen, but what really caught his eye was the icon used in the carmaker's logo. It seemed to finish off the car perfectly. The car would not look nearly as great without it. As he stared at the car, he realized that the icon seemed to encompass the spirit of the car, defining it in a way that words could not. Moreover, the icon was recognized the world over.

*That's it!* he thought excitedly. *I need to create icons like the ones used on cars. Simple drawings that are powerful in their message, that capture the essence of the elements that give us our powers. If I do a good job, maybe one day they will be as widely recognized as the car icons!*

He was so excited that he began grinning about it all.

Marco looked at him curiously and asked, "Why are you so happy?"

"It's just a photo—that car's not actually yours," joked one of the guys, making everyone laugh.

Franco realized he was grinning inanely at a picture of a car and must have looked quite silly. He laughed along with the guys so he wouldn't lose face. He shook his head. "I was just imagining myself driving it, and it was really cool. You had better all be nice to me if you want a ride in my fancy sports car one day," he joked as he gave the magazine back to Marco.

"Well, *adios amigos*," he said as he set his skateboard down. "Got to get home now. Catch you later," he shouted as he pumped the ground with his foot and took off. He flew as fast as he could, anxious to get home and start drawing.

His friends kept on laughing as Franco sped off, and Marco said, "That Franco is really something else, but if any of us end up with a car like that one day, it'll be him!"

Franco arrived home, breathless, excited, and full of ideas to start working on. He ran straight up to his room, leaned his skateboard against the wall, opened his box of paints, and laid out all the colors and brushes. He made space on the floor for a big sheet of white paper and started to experiment with different ways to draw the icons. He was full of creativity and couldn't wait to share these ideas with the group.

Tara decided to take her dogs to her favorite dog park. While they played, she sat under the tree where she usually read. But this time, instead of a book, she had brought a pad of paper and a pencil to start thinking about a name for the team. She started with words related to the environment, like "saving the earth," "green," "climate change," and so on. She jotted them all down on her pad, then tapped the pencil against the side of her head while she thought.

She started to think up new names like "The Four Elements," "The Responsibles," "Environmental Heroes," and "Green Team," but wasn't convinced that any of them truly represented who they were or what they were going to do. They were the obvious names, and a little on the corny side. She wanted something absolutely amazing, but kept drawing a total blank. She began to feel frustrated because she was running out of time before she met the group on Monday, and didn't want to be the only one who hadn't done her share.

As she watched her dogs, she heard a guy say to his girlfriend, "Let's put Zoe on her leash now and go grab lunch at Sustina across the street. They have some great organic vegetarian food, and I'm starving."

Tara knew the restaurant well, and really liked going there with her mom. It was one of the few places that allowed you to bring your dog inside, provided it was on a leash. The name Sustina stuck in her mind and she started to play with that word in her head. Suddenly a big grin spread across her face as she figured it out. *That's it! We'll be called "The Sustainables!"*

She was so excited that she quickly wrote it down on her pad in big bold letters so she wouldn't forget. Still smiling, she thought, *I like it. I can't wait to share it with the group to see what they think.*

● ● ● ●

Monday afternoon finally arrived and the heroes met at the totem pole. Mizu, Arielle, and Tara each brought snack food and placed it on one of the nearby wooden tables. Franco arrived a few minutes later and felt a bit strange when he saw all the food. He wasn't the type of guy who carried snacks around. Looking at the food, his tummy gave a loud and uncomfortable growl.

Arielle motioned for him to sit next to her on the bench and he beamed. *All the ladies come around eventually,* he thought, feeling very pleased with himself until Arielle said, "Sit here. There isn't any space on the other side."

Well, at least he'd get to sit by her, he thought—even if the reason wasn't romantic.

As Mizu, Arielle, and Tara took some of the food, they began to chat.

"Where's Birdie?" Tara asked Arielle.

"Probably running late," Arielle replied. "Since I can't take her to school anymore, she has to find things to keep herself busy until I get home. She is so enjoying being able to fly everywhere now, and sometimes she loses track of time while she's out exploring. She'll be along soon. Let's just start."

"All right," Tara said. "Who wants to go first?"

In the momentary silence that followed her question, Mizu, Arielle, and Tara heard Franco's tummy growling loudly.

Tara giggled. "Franco," she said, "you don't have to wait for an invitation. Please help yourself. Here, try one of these cookies. I baked them with my mom last night." And before Franco could protest, Tara had shoved one into his hand. Franco took a big bite and sighed in approval.

"Mmmm … These are good, Tara," he mumbled through a mouth full of cookie.

Tara smiled, then turned to Mizu. "I think you should go first. Your idea will unite us as one, which Mother Nature said is the crux of the mission."

Mizu swallowed hard. He was happy with what he had invented, but wasn't very good at reading people and had no idea how they would react. He just knew he would be really upset if they hated the watches, and wasn't sure how many more blows his fragile self-esteem could take.

Very slowly and nervously, he reached down into his backpack, pulled out the sketches of the watches and laid them on the table. He then explained how they will function. When he had finished, he turned to Arielle and said, "The only thing I need to finish them is the outfits you designed. I'll need your help to work them into each of the apps. That will keep us from being recognized."

"Mizu, *amigo*, these are fantastic!" Franco said, leaning over the table to high-five Mizu and snatch one more of Tara's cookies.

"Way cool," Tara agreed with a big smile. "Good job, Mizu!"

Arielle grinned. "You've outdone yourself. I knew you were good at science, but these are amazing! They will be the perfect accessory to our outfits!"

"Do you have those done already?" Tara asked.

"Well, not exactly," Arielle admitted. "I wanted to get your opinions about the colors I've chosen before I start designing. And now I'm glad I didn't, because I need to work with Mizu to put them into the app. #ModernTechnologyRocks!"

Arielle pulled four pieces of fabric from her backpack and laid them on the table. It had been quite a challenge to find fabric swatches the exact color of her friends' dresses, but she had managed to do it.

"These colors represent who we are and what we stand for," she said. "Purple will be mine because it feels fresh and airy like me. Personally I love purple, so it will represent me and my air powers. And it will look great against my complexion.

Tara winced and looked over at Arielle, who clearly hadn't realized what she had just said. *Did she just imply she's an airhead?* Tara giggled to herself.

As usual, Arielle was so absorbed in her own talking that she didn't notice Tara looking at her strangely. She held up a bright red swatch. "I think this will be great for you, Franco. The color is strong like your personality, and totally fits with you and your fire element."

Franco was amazed at Arielle's insight, and thought, *maybe there is more to Arielle than meets the eye. She isn't just a pretty face, but is creative too.*

"I like it," he said as he reached for still another of Tara's cookies.

Then Arielle showed them the deep green fabric. "This will be for you, Tara. It complements your pretty green eyes and represents the power of the earth better than any other color."

Tara felt a little ashamed for having had mean thoughts about Arielle earlier, and thought she might not be so bad after all. *She just takes some getting used to.*

Tara smiled and said, "I love this color. It reminds me of fresh grass."

"Yes, I know," Arielle replied excitedly. "I totally see you in this color."

She held up the last piece of fabric. The nice, soft turquoise blue reminded them all of the sea. Mizu looked at her and said, "I guess this is for me, right?"

"Yes, Mizu," Arielle confirmed. "This color represents your water power. It's soft and flowing and reminds me of the ocean, which makes it a perfect fit for you."

Mizu smiled. "You're right. I like it. Thanks so much, Arielle, you did a great job with this. I'm glad you're going to help me with the app so we can make these colors come alive in our costumes. Let's meet up this week to put all your designs into the apps."

Arielle was super-excited. She hadn't expected such an enthusiastic reaction to fabric swatches from a jock, a science geek, and an earth child, and was really glad that she could make a meaningful contribution to the group's efforts to become a team. She hated knowing that the others viewed her as a dumb cheerleader with no brains—even if nobody said it out loud. Maybe now they'd start taking her seriously.

"Great!" said Arielle. "Can't wait to work on it."

Franco turned to Arielle and said, "Great presentation and great color matches for each of us. You really got it. They'll be a perfect fit for the symbols I designed for us."

Arielle basked in the praise.

Franco turned to Mizu and said, "If you all like what I've done, you should take my sketches home so you can use them in the apps."

"Great idea," said Mizu. "Show us what you've got."

Franco pulled the sketches out of his bag. "So, this is mine," he said as he showed them a drawing of a flame so intricate and detailed that it looked real. "I'm responsible for fire, so I thought I'd create a flame icon to represent my power."

Four Become One

"Wow! Great sketch, Franco," said Arielle. "It's perfect for you. Show mine now. I can't wait any longer."

Franco held up the sketch for Arielle's icon. "Yours was actually the hardest, Arielle. How do you draw air?"

Arielle looked worried until he turned the paper around to show her what he had created.

"Umm, why did you draw a snake for me?" Arielle asked with a slight scowl on her face.

"What snake? Where do you see that?" Franco asked defensively.

"It looks like a coiled-up snake," she replied, pointing to the drawing.

"Oh, I get it," Franco said, laughing. "You're funny, Arielle. This isn't a snake. I created the spiral of a funnel cloud for you because you have such a strong personality, and cyclones are some of the strongest forces of air on earth. I thought it was the perfect way to represent your power."

"Oh, right. Now I see it," she said, embarrassed. *I have got to start thinking before I open my mouth,* she chided herself silently, then excitedly continued. "#LoveIt! I can't wait to see it on my costume."

"Glad you like it," said Franco, grinning broadly. "I can't wait, either."

Then he showed them Tara's icon. "Yours was also pretty tough, Tara, because I didn't know the best symbol to represent the power of Earth. I started out trying to design a tree. It just wasn't working, so in the end I decided on this."

He turned the paper around to reveal a beautiful leaf.

Tara just stared at the paper, not saying a word, her eyes filling up with tears. Franco felt his mouth go dry. *Oh God, she hates it,* he thought. *I knew she was going to be the toughest one to please, but*

*I really thought I'd nailed it with this drawing. It's not so terrible that she needs to cry about it. I'll do another one. Geez!*

He said, "I'm sorry you don't like it, Tara. As I said, it was a tough one and I couldn't think of anything else. I'll go back and try again. Please stop crying."

"No, Franco, you don't understand. I'm not crying because I'm upset. I just got emotional from your design," Tara explained. "The place I feel most relaxed is when I'm up in a tree, surrounded by hundreds of leaves. This is really beautiful. It's perfect for me. Thank you."

Franco breathed a sigh of relief and smiled at her. "Oh, wow! I'm so glad you like it."

He turned to Mizu. "Now, Mizu, are you ready, *amigo?*"

Mizu laughed. "I sure am!"

Franco showed them his last sketch, which depicted two waves. "I created the waves icon for you because they best represent the powerful force of water."

Mizu looked at it with a big smile on his face. "I love it! It's perfect. Thanks so much for all your hard work. These icons will look great on our costumes. I really can't wait to see it all put together now. I'm really excited to get these apps finished."

Franco felt so proud that they all loved his drawings. He relaxed now that his presentation was over, and grabbed yet another cookie.

Now it was time for Tara to tell them her ideas. She wiped away her happy tears, excited to share her part with the group. "Ok, guys, sorry I got so emotional. I think everything that has happened lately just caught up with me. I'm excited to be a part of this, but it can be really overwhelming at times."

They all nodded in agreement.

"It was really hard for me to come up with the perfect name," Tara continued. "But I think I finally found the right one."

"Come on, Tara, just tell us," Arielle blurted out. "I can't stand the suspense anymore. Patience is not my thing!"

Franco stared expectantly at Tara with a mouth full of cookies, waiting to hear her idea for their new name.

Sitting next to her, Mizu nudged her gently with his elbow and said, "Go ahead, Tara."

"Right," she said. She was more nervous than she cared to admit. This was big. This was their name. It was how the whole world would come to define them as they undertook their mission.

"So, from now on we will be known as…the Sustainables." She threw the name out there and waited.

Everyone was quiet.

"Do you hate it?" she asked, dreading the answer.

"No," said Mizu. "It sounds cool, but something's missing. I just can't put my finger on it.

"Yeah," Arielle agreed. "It needs a bit more oomph, you know?"

Tara frowned. *Oomph?* she thought. *What the heck does that mean?*

Mizu, looking at Tara's expressionless face and feeling sorry for her, said, "We like it, but we need to add something to it to make it a stronger, more forceful name."

"Franco," Arielle said, "you want to stop eating cookies for a minute and help us out here?"

Franco gulped. "Tara, first I want to tell you that your cookies are *super, super* good. I can't stop eating them."

Mizu and Arielle looked at each other and jumped up at the same time. "That's it, we'll be the Super Sustainables!" they shouted.

"Thanks so much, Franco!" Mizu said quickly. "That was all you!"

Franco looked at them with a weird look on his face, uncertain about what had just happened. But he liked the sound of the new name for the team.

"*Yeah!*" shouted Tara. "That's a much better name!"

The new heroes were so excited that they were whooping and high-fiving one another when Birdie flew up.

"I can hear you on the other side of the park," Birdie pointed out. "You might want to keep your voices down about all this hero stuff, and try to act like a normal group of kids."

"But that's just it," Arielle replied, grabbing Birdie and giving her a big hug. "We're *not* just a group of normal kids anymore. We're the Super Sustainables."

Birdie looked at them, considering the name. "The Super Sustainables, huh? That sounds like a great team name. Good job, guys."

She turned to Arielle. "It sounds like I've missed a lot. Shall we head home and you can fill me in?"

"For sure," Arielle replied.

"Great meeting, and good work, everyone," said Franco as the meeting concluded. "Let's meet again next Monday to check out our new Super Sustainables watches."

They gathered up their things and headed home, feeling happier about everything for the first time since meeting Mother Nature.

Chapter 9

# High-Tech Makeover

The following weekend, Arielle went to Mizu's house to finalize the costumes. She was glad she didn't have to sew them by hand. While she had an eye for fashion and a flair for design, she was rather hopeless with a needle and thread. She was super-excited to see how they would be created through the app Mizu had developed for them to activate their powers. She considered herself to be quite tech-savvy and loved using new technology and apps on her phone, but had never heard of something like this before. She couldn't wait to see how it all worked.

Mizu had invited her over at a time when he knew his parents would be out. He wasn't ready to field a lot of awkward questions he wouldn't be able to answer. The truth was, he wasn't quite sure how his parents would react to having a friend there. He had never invited anyone to his home before. Most of his "friendships" were online or on his WhatsApp science chat group. He figured his mom would be so overexcited to see a pretty and popular girl like Arielle visiting him that she would probably say something to embarrass him.

Mizu was still cementing his status with his hero friends, and wasn't prepared to jeopardize that just yet.

He opened the door and invited Arielle inside. He took her up to his room, which was littered with lots of high-tech gadgets he had taken apart in order to build new ones, books, wires/cables, tools, and other things.

As she took it all in, Arielle noticed a small table pushed into the corner behind the door that had something on it covered by black fabric. She thought the shape looked peculiar, but couldn't tell what it was.

"Interesting room you've got here. I thought I had a lot of stuff, but you win the prize."

"Yeah, sorry about the mess. I've got a few projects I'm experimenting with at the moment."

Then Arielle pointed to the table with the strangely shaped object covered by black fabric. "What's that thing over there on the table? It's really big."

Mizu nervously responded, "Oh that? It's nothing." He paused for a moment and then continued, "It's something I've been working on for about two years, but I'm not ready to talk about it yet. How about we get started on our costumes? That's why you're here, right?" He smiled timidly.

Arielle could tell that he was hiding something, but decided not to push for more details because she was really excited to start working on the costumes.

Mizu explained how the apps worked. "You can design the costumes through the apps on the iPad and then I'll upload them to each of the watches," he told her, and left her alone to focus while he continued to work on something else across the room.

Arielle hoped she understood it all. She easily used technology and apps, but wasn't too interested in all of the backend coding. Mizu had promised to help her if she needed it, which put her mind at ease.

She began by working with the colors she'd "found" at the mall, and selected the right fit and style for each of the heroes' costumes. It was a tough job, but Arielle loved fashion and always made sure that her friends looked good. She would never be able to bring herself to hang around someone who wasn't wearing something stylish and looking their best. Now she had three more friends she was going to be spending a lot of time with, and truth be told, she really felt that Mizu and Tara needed some fashion help. *I'm such a fashion snob!* she laughed to herself.

She had already decided that she wouldn't hurt their feelings by bringing up their fashion shortcomings, but would just create amazing costumes that would give them some much-needed style. *How we look is also part of our power, and very important,* she thought. *First impressions can make or break you, and we need to get this right if we are going to succeed on our mission.*

Although she wanted her new friends to look good as heroes, she was most excited about how *she* would look, so she started with her costume. She had fun experimenting with the app, creating a lot of different styles for her dress. One had hearts all over it, while another option was a tight shirt and skinny black pants like Catwoman wore.

But she wasn't really sold on any of those. As she became more comfortable with the app, she played around with the color purple for her costume. In the end, she opted for a cute skirt and sleeveless top and then set about finding the right accessories. She had always wanted a tiara, so she added a sleek silver headband with the spiral tornado symbol Franco had created to represent her element. Mother Nature had also mentioned that she had the ability to fly, so she needed a cape too. After experimenting with a few different color combinations, she designed a long yellow cape that perfectly complemented her outfit.

High-Tech Makeover

When she finished, she was really happy with what she saw. She wished she could see how it would look on her, but knew she needed to wait for Mizu to finish with all the coding.

She moved on to create Franco's costume. She knew his would be easy because he already looked cool. When she was done, he would look even cooler. She chose the color red for his clothes and added a few flames. Since his job was dealing with fire, she decided he needed something strong to protect him and others from getting burned. So she gave him a cool metal shield with his icon on it.

Just as she was about to save it, she remembered that Mother Nature had told him he could jump high and soar through the air. So, she designed a pair of cool shoes to propel him upward and forward. Then she looked at the final outfit critically.

"Hmmm, something's missing," she said to herself. After a few minutes, she was struck with pure genius. *Sometimes I surprise even myself,* she thought with a smile. For the final touch, she decided it'd be fun to style his red hair like flames, and instinctively knew Franco would love this idea. She reviewed what she had created one last time and was thrilled with her work.

"Wow, I am *really* good at this. Even better than I thought," she complimented herself.

Next was Tara. *Both Tara and Mizu will be more challenging,* she thought. *They're both so different from me, and I really want to make them look cooler than they are.* To start, she added some texture to the deep green color she had chosen for Tara so it looked like tree branches. She didn't know Tara that well, but she was very good at reading people. She knew Tara was not the type of girl who would be comfortable in a dress or skirt. She played around with some ideas before eventually settling on a pair of orange shorts with some comfy yet trendy gladiator-style sandals to match. The overall effect showed Tara's strength and courage, while still being fashionable.

As she looked at the outfit, though, she felt it needed something more to take it from being just great to *Wow!* She remembered Mother Nature saying that Tara's powers would come from the special seed she found. Arielle puzzled for a while as to how she could integrate that seed into the costume. Finally, she decided to add a staff to Tara's ensemble. It looked like a flower and she cleverly incorporated Franco's leaf design as well. She was just thinking about how Franco had tried to design Tara a tree icon when an idea popped into her head. *I wonder if that would work,* she thought. *It would definitely make the whole effect far more fun and edgy, but will Tara go for it?*

She went back and forth in her head for a bit before thinking, *Oh well, nothing ventured, nothing gained.* She changed both Tara's hair color and style. A satisfied Arielle smiled as she thought, *Tara's going to look so cool. I hope she's open to a different look. I don't know her that well but I do know she's tough, fights back, and has a strong personality. This new look is very different from how she normally looks, but I'm the one with the eye for fashion. She can take it, leave it, or kill me.*

Last but not least was Mizu. *He's a tough one, too,* thought Arielle as she asked herself what she could do to make such a nerdy guy look cool. She glanced around his room for inspiration, and noticed the aquarium near his bed with a few fish swimming around. Looking over the rest of the room, she saw his knitted hat hanging on the door and his surfboard leaning against the wall.

And that's when she had an idea. She decided to create a cool but kind of crazy look completely opposite to what he was used to wearing. She started with the turquoise color for his clothes and added the texture of waves. Then she gave him flippers for his feet and fins for his arms. And lastly, she created a swimming cap that resembled a plastic snorkel. It would allow him to breathe underwater just like Mother Nature said, and could also be used as a hose to control water when he wasn't swimming.

As she finished, Arielle couldn't stop giggling as she quietly said, "I wish I could see him in this right now."

Mizu heard Arielle giggling and wondered what on earth she was finding so funny. "Everything okay, Arielle? What's so funny?"

"Everything's fine, Mizu," she replied. "I was just imagining something in my head, that's all. I just finished and added everything to the app. Now all you need to do is connect it to our powers and to our apps."

"Great. I can't wait to see what you came up with and how we're going to look," he said excitedly. "I hope you chose something nice for me—but not too crazy. Can I see it?"

"Oh, no, no, no nothing too crazy, don't worry," she answered with a giggle. *Maybe I went too far with my creativity for Tara and Mizu,* she thought, hoping they wouldn't hate what she'd done.

"Let's wait," she suggested, still giggling. "They look good in the apps, but I won't be able to really tell until we try them on."

"Okay, I'm sure we'll look great," said Mizu. "So now all that's left is for me to connect the last few dots so we'll transform into our super selves when we tap the icons Franco drew."

"So how's this all going to work?" asked Arielle.

"Well, it's pretty technical but basically I'm going to set it up so that when we tap on our apps, the energy connects with the elements Mother Nature gave us from the totem pole. This will cause a transformation by activating our powers, and will change us into our super selves wearing the outfits you designed."

"Oh, said Arielle, slightly confused. "You make it sound so easy."

"It is easy when you know how," Mizu said shyly. He was really good at this sort of thing, but wasn't comfortable boasting about his abilities.

"#It'sReallyHappening!" said a giddy Arielle. "We are so close now. How long will it take you to finish the apps, Mizu?"

"I need two days to put everything together, and then we can try it."

"Can't wait," said Arielle, and gave Mizu a spontaneous hug from all the excitement of the day.

Mizu blushed so hard he thought his head might explode from the heat in his face. No girl had ever hugged him before, never mind one as pretty as Arielle.

His happiness quickly disappeared as he heard the front door opening. In a panic, he turned to Arielle and said, "I'm so sorry to be rude, but, umm, you need to leave now so my parents don't see you here. They'll ask me a million questions about you and what we've been doing and why I didn't tell them that you were coming over. Trust me, it will be a really awkward situation."

Arielle looked around in a panic. "Where am I supposed to go without being seen?"

Mizu was in a state of shock and just stood there with his mouth opening and closing like one of the fish in his aquarium, his head moving back and forth between Arielle and the door to his bedroom. They were trapped!

A voice pierced the shocked silence. "Mizu? Mizu, are you here?" It was his mom, and they could hear her footsteps coming up the stairs.

"Quick," Mizu said to Arielle, "hide under my bed or in my closet. My mom's coming!"

Arielle was about to argue that she didn't see what the big deal was about him having a friend over to visit, but then she saw the sheer terror etched all over his face and decided against it. Obviously this was a big deal to him.

"Okay," she replied. "Just get rid of her so I can get out of here, okay?"

Mizu nodded and swallowed hard. Arielle could make out beads of sweat forming along his hairline, and her heart contracted. She had grown really fond of Mizu in the weeks since they had met. It was horrible to see him so upset—even if she couldn't understand the reason.

His mom's footsteps stopped outside his room and she knocked softly. "Mizu, are you in here?" his mom asked.

Mizu's eyes were so wide that Arielle thought they might pop out of his head. He was just staring at her, frozen to the spot. Then his doorknob rattled and his mom began opening the door.

*This is it. I'm done for,* he thought. *Maybe I can convince her that Arielle is just a study buddy.*

He closed his eyes tightly, wanting to believe this was all just a bad dream, but then heard his mom say, "Mizu, are you okay? Why are you standing there like that?"

He slowly opened his eyes and looked at his mom. His father followed her into the room and asked, "Is everything okay up here?"

Mizu quickly turned around to see if Arielle was there, but she had disappeared. *Phew, she must have dived under my bed just in time.*

He looked at his parents' worried faces and nervously stammered, "Umm, I was just meditating. We learned about it in class last week and I thought I would try it to relax. I was feeling a bit tense, so I wanted to see if it worked."

"Okay, Mizu," his mom said. "As long as you're all right." Her gaze went past him, and her brow furrowed in concern.

*Oh no,* Mizu despaired. *What has she seen? The only thing worse than finding a girl in my room, is finding a girl stuffed under the bed in my room. Then she'll really think I'm up to no good.*

His mom looked at him sternly and asked, "Mizu, why is your window open? We have the air conditioner on because it's been so warm. Please close it and then clean up this room. It's a real pigsty in here. What's going on with you?"

"Sorry, Mom," Mizu replied. "I've just been busy with a few inventions. I'll get it cleaned up."

With that, his parents left. As they headed back downstairs, Mizu heard his father ask his mother, "Why would he need to meditate at his age? What could possibly be so stressful?"

His mother answered, "I don't know, but he needs to spend less time alone in his room and get out to be around other kids his age."

When he was sure the coast was clear, Mizu looked under his bed to help Arielle out. She wasn't there. He looked behind his desk and in his closet, but she wasn't there either.

"Arielle, you can come out now," he whispered. "They just left. Where are you?"

He was puzzled when Arielle didn't respond. *How did she just disappear like that? Where could she have gone?*

He walked over to close the window like his mom had asked, and saw Arielle down in the yard, hiding behind a tree.

"Arielle," he whispered loudly.

She poked her head out from behind the tree and waved, a huge grin on her face.

"How did you get down there?"

"I can fly, remember?" Arielle answered with a wink. "I thought it was the perfect time to try it out."

Mizu just hoped nobody had seen her flying—otherwise he would have some serious explaining to do. A much more relaxed and composed Mizu smiled and exhaled in relief. "Now I know this is not a dream," he said to himself as he waved goodbye to Arielle and closed the window.

# High-Tech Makeover

Chapter 10

# Powers United

After another week of hard work, it was time for the new heroes to meet again to see their ideas come to life, and truly become the Super Sustainables for the first time. It was early Monday morning and Birdie started playfully pecking at Arielle's head.

"Wake up, Sleeping Beauty, today is a big day," she said.

"Why are you so loud and why on earth are you pecking at me?" Arielle complained. "Sleeping Beauty woke up with a kiss, not with an obnoxious bird pecking at her head!" she exclaimed as she covered her head with her blanket.

"This *is* me kissing you," Birdie said indignantly. "I've got sharp lips—what can I do?" she added as she flew over to perch on the windowsill.

Arielle was so tired from the busy week and weekend that she just wanted to sleep a little bit more, but Birdie was having none of it. "Come on, Arielle. Wake up, already," she squawked. "You'll be late for school, and we also need to meet the team this afternoon—I hope you haven't forgotten that."

"Okay, okay, stop shouting at me. It was a hard week for me, you know." She stretched one last time, threw back the covers, and climbed out of bed. "So what's my OOTD today?" she asked, referring to her "Outfit of the Day."

After choosing a gorgeous yellow dress and matching shoes, she began to get ready. As she pulled a brush through her long blonde hair, she looked at Birdie and said, "I'm so nervous."

"What are you nervous about?"

"Today we're going to meet again—what if the others don't like the costumes I created for them?"

"They'll love them. Don't worry so much."

"Thanks, Birdie, but I need to share something with you. I may have gone too far."

"Huh? What did you do? Are you in trouble?"

"No, not trouble, just getting cold feet. When designing our outfits, I really pushed my creativity with Tara's and Mizu's. Now I'm starting to feel like they may be too crazy for them. After all, good fashion designers should match the outfit with their client's personality. And with Tara and Mizu, I actually thought more about how to make them cool. Birdie, let's face it, they are *not* cool kids. But if I'm part of this team, I want us all to look great … and, well, cool. Don't you agree?" she asked, hoping Birdie would say yes and put her mind at ease.

Birdie listened… and then started to laugh. "This is *so* you, Arielle. So all this worry is over the outfits you designed for them?"

"Yes. And I changed Tara's hair from brown with pigtails to a green afro, like a tree. And for Mizu, I added fish fins to his bodysuit. Do you think that's too much for them to handle?" she asked nervously, biting her lower lip.

Birdie could not stop laughing. "Green hair? Fish fins? Girl, you did go too far, I think. I can't wait to see how this goes over. Tara is going to freak out!"

"Thanks, Birdie. You really know how to make someone feel better," Arielle replied despondently. "Can I ask you a favor?"

"Sure. You can ask, but doesn't mean I'll do it." Birdie was still chuckling at Arielle's anxiety.

"I'm serious, Birdie," Arielle said, her eyes filling with tears.

Birdie mentally rolled her eyes. Arielle could be so dramatic! But she decided to be nice, and said, "Okay, what can I do for you?"

"This time I really need you to support me and be on my side. When you see the new outfits, please compliment them and don't make fun of me. You've seen how Tara gives me that look—like she's ready to kill me. It's about time we support each other like real friends do." She looked pleadingly at Birdie, and Birdie knew she was right. She had so been enjoying the banter that she forgot how stressful this whole hero business was for Arielle.

"Tara's not going to kill you," she said. "Just relax."

Arielle exhaled in relief. "Thanks, Birdie," she said with a weak smile.

"I mean, she might be a little upset that you gave her green hair, but she won't actually *kill* you," Birdie added teasingly.

Arielle picked a pillow up off her bed and tossed it at Birdie. "Stop it!" she shouted. But she was smiling as she said it.

"Now, all joking aside," Birdie said, "where is your confidence, Miss Fashion Expert?"

But she saw the genuine worry etched on Arielle's face and decided to stop kidding around. She said seriously, "You know you're good at this. Think of all the times you've helped your girlfriends pick out the right outfits. Look at how you've changed Sarah's style. When you first met her, she was also kind of a geek, but you helped her out, and now she looks almost as good as you. You changed her life."

"Hmmm, you're right. I guess I did."

"So, let's wait and see their reactions. To be and look different is not a bad thing. You just need to be open-minded about it."

Arielle started to feel a little better, knowing she had Birdie's support. She chose two pretty clips and started pinning them into her hair before stopping midway, turning to Birdie, and asking, "Hold on. How'd you know about what I did for Sarah? You were just a stuffed toy back when I met her."

"I saw and heard everything. I just couldn't talk or move." She flew over to sit on Arielle's shoulder. "Now stop worrying about something you're totally good at, and go meet your friends. They'll love your outfits!"

"Okay, you're right," said Arielle as she applied some pink lip gloss. She stood up to admire her reflection in the mirror and said with a smile, "I look great! Now I'm ready to face the day."

The day seemed to drag by as the Super Sustainables waited anxiously for the final bell to ring so they could hurry to their meeting at the totem pole.

When they had all finally arrived and said hello to each other, Franco turned to Mizu and exclaimed, "I'm so excited! I can't wait to see what you've done."

Mizu smiled in response and teasingly said, "Oh, was I supposed to bring my invention today? I forgot it at home."

Franco nudged him good-naturedly. "Come on, quit joking around and show us! You're killing me, dude."

Mizu looked around the park to see if they were alone. Even though he couldn't see anybody, he turned to Birdie and said, "Would you mind being the lookout?"

"Why me? Arielle can also fly," Birdie complained.

Arielle looked at Birdie with her hands on her hips and said sarcastically, "Really, Birdie? Yeah, because if people saw a teenage girl flying around the park, it wouldn't attract any attention at all."

"Okay, okay. I get it, but I don't want to miss out on the big reveal!"

"Don't worry," Arielle said kindly. "I'll fill you in on all the details, I promise."

With that, Birdie took off to keep watch.

"Okay, so are you guys ready?" asked Mizu.

"Totally!" they all chorused.

"Before I show you, I just want to say that this is the first time I've ever shown one of my inventions to anyone. Most people just laugh at me and think I'm weird, but you all believed in me. We are all part of this invention—I couldn't have done it without you guys."

"Of course we believe in you," said Tara. "We're a team now, working together."

Mizu looked at her and smiled. "Thanks, Tara," he said. "That means a lot."

"Okay, enough with the lovey-dovey stuff," Franco said impatiently.

"Show us your invention, already."

Mizu looked at Franco and smiled. He didn't know Franco well, but he had never seen the other boy so excited. He was actually bouncing on his toes, unable to keep still, so Mizu decided to put him out of his misery. He reached into his bag and pulled out four watches.

"Here we go," he said, and handed them out. He'd added the final touch the night before, color-coding the wristbands to match the colors Arielle had chosen for each of them.

"#ILoveNewStuff," said Arielle. "These watches are so fashionable, and I love my purple wristband," she said as she placed it over her wrist.

Franco looked disappointed, though. He'd already seen the design, and it didn't look all that special now that he was holding it. "What's so special about these, anyhow?" he asked, battling to hide his disappointment. "They look like normal watches to me."

"Yeah, Mizu, what's so special about them and why is the screen black? How does it work?" asked Tara, trying to diffuse the situation. She could see that Mizu looked upset by Franco's reaction, and thought Franco was being a little unfair. He'd been excited about the watch the week before—why was he suddenly acting like it was the end of the world?

"I promise they're *not* just normal watches," Mizu explained. "I used something ordinary so they wouldn't draw attention to us as we go about our daily activities."

Franco perked up. "But they do cool stuff, right?"

"I wouldn't let the team down," Mizu said with a smile. He was trying to act confident, but he was a bundle of nerves inside. *What if after I've shown them what the watches can do, they still hate them? I worked so hard.*

The other kids all watched him eagerly, waiting for him to tell them what to do. He snapped out of his doubts and decided to go for it.

"Okay, put them on and then turn them on," Mizu instructed.

They all put their watches on, and at Mizu's count, turned the power on.

Facing the Drought

Suddenly, bright lights illuminated the screens with their new name—The Super Sustainables.

"That's so cool," said Franco.

"I love the pretty colors," said Arielle.

Then each of their power icons appeared. "Wow! My icon looks even better on the screen," said Tara.

"Yes, mine too," said Arielle.

Circling high above, Birdie saw the bright colors shining up from where they were standing. What's going on down there? she thought. I hate missing out on all the fun!

"So, what now, Mizu?" asked Franco. "Maybe we should all tap our icons at the same time. We *are* supposed to be a team, so we should do it at the same time, right?"

But Arielle was still a little nervous about how Tara and Mizu would react to their costumes, and with Birdie flying high above them, she couldn't support her like they'd planned. If they tapped their icons, and Mizu was right, they'd all become their superhero personalities. That meant they'd be dressed in the costumes she'd designed. She was no longer sure this was such a good idea.

"Hold on, guys," she said, stalling for time. "What if something happens to me when I tap it? What if I vanish from the planet?"

Mizu smiled and said, "Come on. I explained to you how this works when you were at my house the other day, so you know it's not a magic watch, Arielle. Just a special one." Arielle looked at him and raised her eyebrow. "So scientifically speaking, it's perfectly feasible to have talking birds and flying cheerleaders?" she asked.

"Okay, fine," Mizu relented. "You've made your point, but I promise nothing bad will happen. Now let's see if everything works like I planned. Are you ready?"

"Mizu, can you explain to us how this works? I'd like to know what to expect," said Tara with growing curiosity.

"Sure. Well, like I explained to Arielle, it's pretty technical. Basically, I've set it up so that when we tap on our apps, the energy connects with the power Mother Nature gave us at the totem pole. This will cause a transformation and activate our powers to change us into our super selves—wearing the outfits Arielle designed."

Franco looked at Arielle with what he hoped was a reassuring expression and said, "Don't worry, that doesn't sound too scary. And besides, we'll try it together. If you disappear off somewhere, I'm sure we'll disappear too, so at least we'll all be together. Don't be scared."

Arielle thought it was cute how Franco was trying to make her feel better, but that wasn't what she was *actually* worried about.

"Okay," said Tara. "Let's do this!"

"#MomentOfTruth!" Arielle said.

So, on the count of three, all four heroes tapped their icons to open their new power apps. Suddenly, four bright lights in the heroes' colors burst out of their watches and shone high up into the sky. The four of them stood there speechless, dumbfounded at what was happening.

The lights passed by Birdie, and she shouted down, "What's going on down there? What's with all these bright, colorful lights?"

Arielle's eyes were tightly closed when she heard the other kids oohing and aahing. She waited a few seconds before slowly opening them and immediately looked over at Tara. Without realizing it, she blurted out, "Oh, Tara, your hair is brown."

"I was born with brown hair and have had it all my life," Tara responded with a look of confusion. "Why are you so surprised?"

"Oh, nothing," said Arielle, realizing her faux pas. "I just really like your pretty brown hair."

Tara was still not convinced that Arielle was being sincere, and thought her comment was weird. *I hope the cheerleader isn't losing it from all this stress,* she thought.

Powers United

Then Franco said, "How come we're still ourselves? Weren't we supposed to change into the Super Sustainables costumes, Mizu?"

Mizu was confused as well, and wasn't sure what to say to the three of them staring at him and waiting for an answer. He had also thought they would change into their costumes. That's what he had programmed the app to do when they tapped their icons. Maybe he had made a mistake with the coding or something.

He couldn't believe he'd screwed it up.

"I'm not sure what went wrong," he began. "I'll have to open up the watches and…"

He trailed off as a familiar voice filled the air. "Hello, my four heroes. Did you call me? Is everything alright?"

They looked up, and in the middle of where their four beams of light joined together was Mother Nature. She smiled at them as she floated down from the sky.

The four heroes stood there shocked by her sudden appearance. They had definitely not been expecting to see Mother Nature here today. And they hadn't even realized that they were — somehow — calling her.

"Oh, hi, Mother Nature," Franco said, breaking the silence. "We were just busy trying to figure out how these special watches that Mizu developed for us work."

"I'd say they work quite well," Mother Nature said with a smile.

"Huh?" asked Arielle. "They don't work at all, other than as a huge flashlight!"

"Yeah," said Mizu. "I must have connected the wrong wires or made an error in the coding. I've been working late and I'm exhausted, so I guess I could have gotten something mixed up. I need to get home to figure it out and fix it."

Mother Nature smiled at the looks of confusion on their faces. "The watches aren't broken, Mizu, and they don't need fixing. I told you that you could contact me when you found a way to unite all your powers. And that's what you just did."

Suddenly it all made sense to Mizu. He looked at Mother Nature, then up into the sky with the four beams joined together, and realized what happened. "I think I get it now. Tapping our apps at the same time united the energy from our elements, which must have sent a message to you. But they were *supposed* to activate our powers to change us into our hero personas."

"Correct," Mother Nature replied. "This is the way to contact me when you need me. I knew I could trust you to find the way—you're clever kids. I've been watching you all work so hard over last few weeks. How are you doing?"

"Better, now," said Franco. "Since we last saw you, we've thought about this new reality. We now know how serious it is, and that it's our responsibility to do what we can to help. We each went away and came back with ideas for making us a real team."

"Sounds interesting," said Mother Nature.

"Each of us has worked really hard for this mission," Franco continued. "Arielle created our unique costumes, Mizu created our special watches, I designed each of the symbols to represent our powers, and Tara thought up our team name."

"Your team name?" asked Mother Nature.

"Yes," Tara said, stepping forward. "We will now be known as the Super Sustainables."

"That's a great name," said Mother Nature, smiling. "It perfectly represents your mission. I knew I chose the right kids for this task. You've just proved that working together leads to amazing results. I'm very proud of all of you.

"Since we're all here together, I need to tell you about something that is becoming a big problem here in California, something the Super Sustainables need to keep a close eye on."

"Big problem?" asked Arielle. "What do you mean?"

"Well, I am sure you've noticed that even though it's winter, it's still pretty warm out. And it hasn't rained for quite some time."

"Yeah, you're right," said Arielle. "So hot and sweaty and … gross."

"Yes," echoed Tara. "I've felt it, especially in my flower garden, which is really dry."

"What happened?" asked Franco. "Why is the weather acting so weird?"

"It's called climate change," Mother Nature explained. "California is facing big problems. You see, there is a serious drought and people are not properly aware of how their actions are making the situation worse."

"Drought," repeated Mizu with concern in his voice. "This is our home. We have to do something to help. Mother Nature, tell us how we can fix this."

At that very moment, Birdie zoomed down. "Quick, act normal! Oh…" She trailed off as she noticed Mother Nature standing there. "When did you get here? *How* did you get here?" Birdie babbled on, confused and curious about what she had missed while on guard.

"Good to see you again, Birdie. I'm here because the Super Sustainables called me," Mother Nature explained.

"Called you? How?" asked Birdie.

"I'll explain it all to you later," said Arielle.

"Why did you come down here, Birdie?" asked Mizu.

"Oh, yes." Birdie tried to regain her focus. "I just wanted to tell you guys that a big group of kids are on their way over here to play in the park. You may want to wrap this up, especially since Mother Nature is here."

"But hold on," said Arielle. "She can't go yet. What should we do about the drought?" she asked, turning to Mother Nature.

Mother Nature looked at Arielle and said, "The answer is *you*. The Super Sustainables. Now I must go. You guys have a lot to think about." Before they could answer, she waved goodbye and disappeared.

"Bummer, man!" Franco exclaimed. "Now we can't check out our costumes."

"Yeah," agreed a disappointed Tara. "I was so excited to see what you came up with, Arielle."

"Never mind," said Arielle quickly. "You'll get to see them next time. I hope you'll like what I chose for you. B-T-W, have you ever colored your hair?" she asked, trying to get a feel for how Tara was going to react.

Tara noticed Arielle was acting even more oddly than usual today with all these questions about her hair. *I hope she's not planning to make me blonde like her,* she thought. "I like my brown hair and I don't have plans to change it any time soon," she told Arielle in a threatening tone of voice.

Arielle looked over at Birdie and whispered, "That's it, she is going to kill me!"

Mizu stepped up. "Guys, I'm sorry about today. I think we need to tap our apps at different times in order to transform into our super selves, but at least now we know how to call Mother Nature. I guess we should get going before those kids get here. We have a lot to think about. And remember, we can also use the watches like cell phones to communicate with each other, by text message or group chat. Kind of like you do with your friends, Arielle. Okay?"

"SustainaWatch!" Tara blurted out.

"What?" asked Mizu, confused.

"I think we should call our new watches the SustainaWatch."

"That sounds cool," agreed Franco. "You're really good at coming up with the right names, Tara."

"Thanks," she responded, clearly delighted by the compliment.

"You know," Franco continued, "speaking of names … I was hoping to get all of your opinions on something."

"What is it?" Mizu asked.

"Well, even before the Super Sustainables came along, I really loved fire. You all know I have Latino blood too, right?"

"Yeah," Tara and Arielle answered.

"Well, the Spanish word for fire is *fuego*, and I was thinking it might be kind of cool to change my name to 'Fuego' when I activate my powers. What do you guys think?"

"I think that's really clever," Arielle said. "What's 'air' in Spanish? I want to change my name, too," she said excitedly.

"It's *aire*," Franco told her.

Arielle frowned. "Oh, really? Are you sure it's just *aire*? Nothing else? That doesn't sound cool enough for me." She crossed her arms, pursed her lips and tapped her forehead with her pointer finger as she said to herself, "think Arielle think."

Birdie pecked Arielle on the ear. "Sometimes you can be such a dumb blonde."

"What?" asked Arielle, confused, as she rubbed her sore ear.

"Say your name really slowly," Birdie went on. "Air–ree–elle. See, your name already has the word 'air' in it."

"Ah, Birdie!" Arielle gushed. "I didn't even *think* about that. You're so right! I'll keep my name as it is, I think. After all, it's a really great name."

"You do know you can't claim the credit for having a great name," Birdie said. "Your parents named you, remember?"

While Birdie and Arielle bickered, Mizu was lost in thought. After a few moments he turned to Tara and said, "You should change your name, too."

"What? Why? What's wrong with my name?" Tara asked, immediately on the defensive. It was one thing having to deal with the cheerleader's comments, but Mizu was a nerd like her. She couldn't understand why he was suddenly being mean.

"Nothing's wrong with Tara, silly," Mizu said, laughing. "It's a lovely name. I was just thinking that maybe you should be called 'Terra' when you activate your powers."

He paused, waiting for them to catch on. When nobody spoke, he continued, "You know, from the Latin word meaning 'of the earth.'"

A broad smile spread across Tara's face. "I get it now. I love it! I'm definitely going to use it. Thanks, Mizu."

"But what about you, Mizu?" Arielle asked with a concerned look on her face. "We all have names relating to our elements, but you don't. Would you like us to help you think of a name?"

"No thanks," said Mizu with a cheeky grin. "I already have the perfect name."

He enjoyed their puzzled expressions for a few moments longer. "Mizu means 'water' in Japanese. I've never told anyone this before, but my real name is 'Mitsue' and it means 'the light' in Japanese. My mom said she gave me the nickname Mizu when I was a baby because I loved the water so much, and it just kind of stuck."

"That's awesome!" exclaimed Arielle.

"Great name, *amigo*," said Franco, patting Mizu on the shoulder.

Tara just beamed, happy that they all had special and meaningful names.

Then, hearing the sounds of the kids getting closer, the four friends said their goodbyes and headed home.

Chapter 11

# Facing the Drought

A few days later, as the Super Sustainables were getting ready for school, each of them heard something they wouldn't ordinarily have given a second thought. None of them had ever been big followers of the news, but it seemed that much had changed since meeting Mother Nature. What they heard reminded them that what she had told them was true.

Franco heard it over the car radio as his dad drove him to school on his way to an early morning meeting.

Tara unexpectedly overheard her neighbors' conversation about the news, while walking her dogs before going to school.

Mizu heard it on his computer. He was logged on to the science channel, but his regular broadcast was interrupted.

Arielle heard it on the flat-screen television in her bedroom while she was deciding which dress to wear by trying them all on and taking selfies. Birdie had been trying to sleep in a bit, but the TV disturbed her and made her feel more than a little grumpy.

"Arielle, what are you doing? And do you have to make so much noise doing it?"

Arielle answered in a chipper tone, "I can't decide what to wear, so I'm trying on all my options and seeing which one takes the best selfie. Why are you so crabby?"

Birdie grumbled, "Just because you have to go to school doesn't mean I have to get up!" And just to make sure Arielle knew she was annoyed, she delivered the final biting comment: "And by the way, you should think twice about that outfit!"

Arielle stood wide-eyed in shock as Birdie pulled the covers back over her head.

"Breaking news! For the past five years, California has been in an extreme and now exceptional drought, which has been made worse by the effects of climate change," the newscaster began. "As a result, the governor of California has ordered a mandatory 25 percent reduction in water use. This obviously has huge impacts on agriculture, industry, and lifestyle…"

The four kids listened to the reporter explaining the effects of the drought. Each had different pieces of information jump out at them.

Tara's attention was drawn to the reports about crop failure due to lack of water, land erosion, and threats to wildlife habitats.

Franco was mesmerized by news of a new wildfire raging near the outskirts of the city. It was thought to have been started by careless hikers. The city was on high alert, and nearby residents were being told to evacuate their homes because firefighters were not certain they would get it under control anytime soon.

Arielle was thinking about how wind could speed up erosion in a dry climate and cause fires to spread more rapidly. Without enough water, uncontrolled fires, aided by strong winds, would pose a threat to all living things—people and animals alike.

Mizu noted the mandatory water reductions. He heard that some towns in California had already run out of ground water and had to rely on imported water delivered by trucks.

"Clearly this is becoming a serious issue, adversely affecting more and more people and jeopardizing the California lifestyle that we all know and love," the newscaster ended. "It's a lot to think about, folks, and we are going to have to do something before it's too late."

The four of them arrived at their respective schools in somber moods, the task ahead weighing heavily on their minds. Each of them found a quiet place and opened the chat app on their SustainaWatches. They were all bursting to talk to someone who understood how serious the situation really was.

Hey guys, did you hear the news?

I sure did. It is all over the Internet.

Me too. I never paid too much attention to the news until today. 😁

Yeah, I tried to listen but Birdie 🐦 was annoying me all morning while I was busy deciding what to wear.

I got to school and all the sprinklers were on. I wanted to just run and turn them all off.

Well, grass does need water to grow, but should only be watered twice a week. I'm sure they'll be switched off soon.

**Facing the Drought**

< Chats

Hope you're right, Mizu.

I saw my friends spraying other kids with the drinking fountain water. They all thought it was SO funny.

That's not right!

Yeah, I know.

People just don't get it, do they?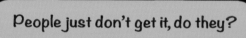

No, I guess they don't.

We were the same until two days ago. I used to think spraying people with the water fountain was a great prank, but now I don't.

Well, when I got to school today, the fire hydrant on our curb was gushing water everywhere. It was, like, such a waste.

OMG! What happened?

Yeah, that sounds awful.

My friend's older brother took his dad's car out for a spin and crashed it right into the fire hydrant. There was a river of water flowing down the street. #LearnToDrive.

Kids are just not thinking before they do stuff. Did we just notice all of this now because we know Mother Nature? And did we all used to be this bad?

Don't be so hard on yourself, Franco. We just know what to look for now.

What do you mean?

I mean, I knew we were in a drought because we had been told about it at school. But I didn't realize how serious it was, or how this could really change our lifestyle—and not for the better. 😔 😢

If we don't start conserving water soon, the world is going to be in big trouble...

Arielle, why do you keep changing your photo every minute? What are you doing over there?

Birdie and I took selfies in my room the other day, 🤳 🤍 🐤 🤍 📱 and I can't decide which one to use for my profile on our chat. 🤔 🤔 🤔

• • • •

As the day went on, Tara got more and more agitated. She kept looking out the windows of her classrooms, and every time she did, she saw the sprinklers still running.

"How careless," she fumed. "There's no need to have them on all day."

When she headed to her last class of the day, she spotted the school custodian.

"Mr. Lawson," she called. "Hey, wait up."

He stopped and turned to look at Tara. "What's up?" he asked.

"Well," Tara began, "I've noticed that the sprinklers have been on all day. And I heard on the news about how serious this drought really is, so they should be turned off!"

Mr. Lawson roared with laughter. "Oh my goodness. Why are you worrying about such things? You're just a kid—go hang out with your friends. A little bit of water here and there is not going to make any difference at all."

Tara tried again. "But every little bit helps." Mr. Lawson hurried off down the hallway, still laughing at her.

Tara walked to her locker in a little bit of shock. She couldn't believe people didn't realize how serious the situation was. All the more reason why it was imperative for her and her team to *get* to people and tell them how important it was — before it was too late.

• • • •

"Hey, Franco," Dave shouted as Franco tried to hurry past him on his way to class. "What's wrong with you today? You taught us how to spray people with the drinking fountains, and now you're yelling at us about it?

"Yeah, I know. I guess I just don't think it's funny to waste water during a drought," Franco replied.

"You need to lighten up, man," Dave called after him. "It's just a bit of fun."

*Humph,* thought Franco crossly. *We'll see how much fun it is when there's no water left for us.*

All day he grew increasingly more concerned as he saw faucets left on in the bathrooms and running toilets in need of repair. The final straw came at football practice when his teammates had a water fight to cool down. Franco went to the locker room to take a quick shower, change, and head home.

He was so disappointed in himself for not seeing it before—but at least now his eyes were wide open. He silently vowed to make a difference…somehow.

●●●●

After gym class, Arielle was in the locker room sitting on the bench. While she loved exercising, she always felt so gross afterwards when she saw how sweaty she got.

"I really need to take a shower before I start to smell bad! #StinkingIsGross!" she said to herself. When she got into the shower area, she saw three showers running with nobody using them. Three girls were standing around gossiping and giggling while the water continued to rain out of the shower heads and a few other girls had left the sink faucets running while they fixed their hair in the mirror. And there were even faucets left running because the girls who had used them forgot to turn them off. Nobody seemed to notice or even care about the amount of water they were wasting.

*Gosh*, Arielle suddenly thought. *Mother Nature wasn't kidding. This whole thing is, like, totally for real and I have to help find a way to fix this mess.*

Without further thought, Arielle started turning off the faucets.

# Facing the Drought

"Arielle, what are you doing?" Sarah asked. "The janitor will do all that later. Come on. And did you ever get a new phone?" she continued.

"New phone?" repeated Arielle, confused. "Oh, right. Sure did."

"Cool, so check your phone," continued Sarah. "We just got a message about a new shop that's opening today. We're going to check it out now. Huge opening sales! You coming?"

"Nah," replied Arielle. "I think I'm just going to head home."

"Really? It's not like you to pass up an opportunity to shop. Is everything okay? You've been acting so weird lately."

"Everything's fine," said Arielle, feeling a little miffed. "I just have other stuff to do. There's more to life than shopping, you know!"

She picked up her stuff and marched out of the locker room, still wearing her stinky, sweaty gym clothes, without so much as a backward glance.

● ● ● ●

Sarah stood staring, her mouth wide open in shock. She knew Arielle very well, and knew she wouldn't ordinarily miss out on an opening sale. Furthermore, the Arielle she knew would rather die than be seen outside of gym class all sweaty and without make up! *I wonder what's up with her,* Sarah thought.

● ● ● ●

Mizu hurried down the hall after his last class, his mind still deeply troubled by what he had heard on the news that morning. He just couldn't seem to get the thought of the drought out of his head. He was so deep in thought that he hardly noticed Max Prodigus, Jr. with his two younger twin brothers, Lance and Rudy, handing out flyers in the schoolyard. Max Jr. was in some of Mizu's classes, so they knew each other, but weren't friends. Max Jr.'s twin brothers were four years younger than Mizu, but he knew of them because of their notorious reputation in their elementary school. They were the resident mischief-makers, who enjoyed teasing the other kids by playing pranks and practical jokes on them.

Mizu found he didn't really have that much in common with Max Jr., so he was quite surprised when Rudy shoved a piece of paper at him. Mizu took it, but between trying to get home on time and worrying about the water problems facing California, he just slipped it into his notebook absentmindedly.

As he was leaving school, he saw Dylan, the guy he'd fought with a few weeks earlier, in the distance hanging out with his friends in the schoolyard. Mizu tried not to make eye contact with him and continued to walk quickly toward the gate.

But it wasn't to be.

"Hey, dork. Is that you?" shouted Dylan.

Mizu heard Dylan's voice but pretended he hadn't and kept walking toward the gate.

"Hey, I'm talking to you, nerd!" Dylan continued. Mizu stopped and turned around. "Oh, it is really you, I think we have some unfinished business," Dylan said, sneering.

Mizu remained frozen, but mustered up the courage to say, "Yes, I remember you."

"You still need to pay for what you did to my girlfriend. Get over here and let's finish this up!"

The laughter from Dylan's friends encouraged him to keep going.

Mizu remained frozen in position and Dylan repeated, "I said come here—now!"

At that moment, like the other day in the hall, more kids started noticing that there might be a fight and headed toward them to see what was going on.

Mizu remained still, watching as the other kids formed a semi-circle around them.

Dylan was growing ever more impatient with Mizu, and said, "Okay, if you're not coming here, then I'll come to you, and you will pay double!"

At that, the other kids and Dylan's friends started to shout, "Fight, fight, fight!" Dylan charged toward Mizu. Everyone around them cheered him on.

Mizu tried to think about what to do. He noticed that the janitor was cleaning the windows with a bucket full of soapy water. Without another thought, Mizu took control of the water in the bucket and caused it to knock itself over. Continuing to use his power over water, he brought a stream of the dirty, soapy water toward himself. Dylan picked up speed, not noticing the soapy water. When he hit it, he came to a hard landing and slid across the schoolyard.

"*Ouch!*" he shouted. "I think I broke something! Man, that hurts."

All the kids waiting for a big fight started laughing at Dylan. In fact, some recorded him with their phones and later posted it on YouTube.

With Dylan lying on the ground helpless, he no longer seemed so scary and intimidating. Mizu slowly moved toward him to give him a hand, because he knew how it felt to be laughed at. But Dylan just shouted, "Leave me alone! I don't need your help, dork. I can do it myself." He tried to stand up on his own, but couldn't because of the pain.

Mizu understood that Dylan's ego was too big to ever accept help from a geek like him. More importantly, he understood that Dylan was not likely to mess with him anymore after this humiliation. A relieved Mizu picked up his things and headed home.

When he got home, Mizu remembered he'd been given something just before his encounter with Dylan. He opened his notebook to see what it was…and was shocked at what he read.

He quickly snapped open his SustainaWatch and left a text for the other Super Sustainables.

**THE SUPER SUSTAINABLES**
MESSAGES

Hello guys, are you there?

Must meet ASAP. Big trouble.

Tomorrow – after school meet me at the totem pole!

THE SUPER SUSTAINABLES
YOU CAN BE A HERO TOO

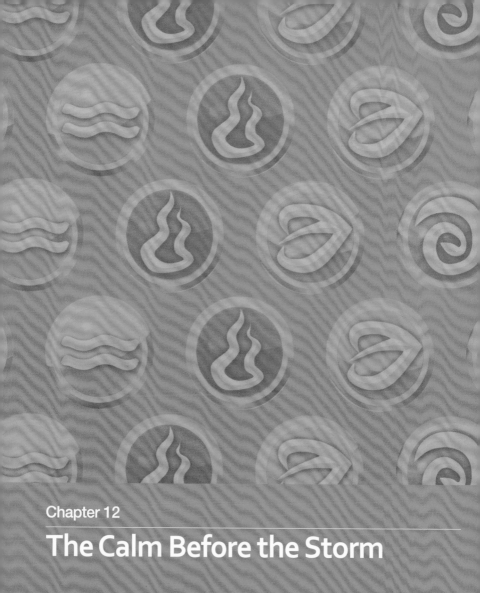

Chapter 12

# The Calm Before the Storm

Mizu was the first one at the park the next afternoon. He sat on the bench, staring up at the totem pole and hoping he would suddenly be struck with inspiration. He clutched the piece of paper tightly in his hand. This was going to be a disaster!

Then he heard footsteps and looked to his left to see Arielle on her way with Birdie. Looking to his right, he saw Tara, and straight ahead, Franco was also approaching. They all sat down and began talking. The awkwardness between them was gone now, and they were all curious about what was so urgent.

"Thanks for coming guys. Any updates?" asked Mizu.

"I couldn't believe it," Tara exclaimed. "The sprinklers ran the whole day and when I asked about turning them off, I got laughed at!"

"I know what you mean," Franco said. "I also ran into trouble when I tried to point out about how important it was not to waste water on practical jokes. I used to enjoy them, but not anymore."

"Yeah," Arielle agreed, "I didn't have much luck, either. After gym class, I went to the locker room totally sweaty, feeling all gross and—"

Birdie interrupted. "T-M-I, Arielle. Get to the point!"

"Oh," said Arielle, realizing she was focusing on the wrong thing. "So, I saw girls in the locker room leaving the sink faucets and showers running while they chatted and gossiped."

The three kids traded stories of all the waste they had seen over the past few days at school and at home, but Mizu remained quiet.

"The part that really gets to me," said Tara, "is that people just don't seem to care. They don't think it's their responsibility."

"Yeah," said Arielle. "I totally agree. My friends don't think what they do can make a difference. They're, like, in total denial, focused only on themselves and completely unaware that they left the faucets running."

"Focused on themselves... Maybe that's something they learned from you," added Birdie — after flying to a safe distance, out of Arielle's reach.

Arielle shot her a mean look through narrowed eyes before flipping her blonde hair over her shoulder and sitting down to examine her nails. As she stared at her latest manicure, she leaned back against the bench and said, "I honestly don't know how the four of us are going to be able to make any difference. I mean, I'm popular, but I'm not like world famous! Well, not yet anyway…"

Tara looked at her with exasperation, "Well, we're going to have to figure it out, Arielle," she said. "We can't just sit around looking at our nails and doing nothing!"

"Hey, dude," said Franco, looking at Mizu. "You okay, *amigo*? You haven't said much since we got here. What's this meeting all about?"

Mizu looked at the three of them and shook his head. "It's terrible," he replied. "Far worse than I thought. The Super Sustainables are facing their first real crisis."

"What do you mean, Mizu?" Tara asked kindly. She was very good at reading people and had noticed how tense he was.

He just handed her the flyer and sat back down while the three of them huddled together to read it.

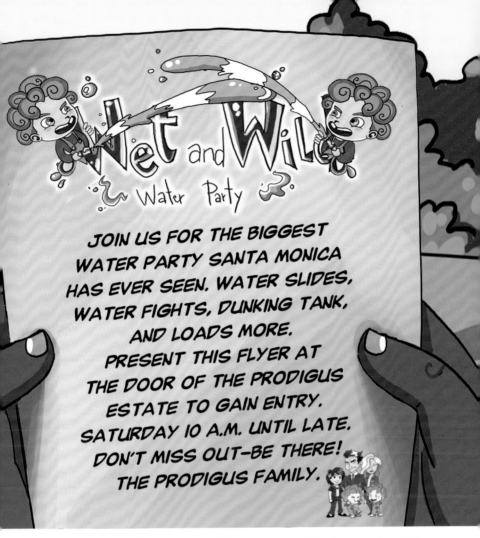

**WET and WILD**
**Water Party**

JOIN US FOR THE BIGGEST
WATER PARTY SANTA MONICA
HAS EVER SEEN. WATER SLIDES,
WATER FIGHTS, DUNKING TANK,
AND LOADS MORE.
PRESENT THIS FLYER AT
THE DOOR OF THE PRODIGUS
ESTATE TO GAIN ENTRY.
SATURDAY 10 A.M. UNTIL LATE.
DON'T MISS OUT—BE THERE!
THE PRODIGUS FAMILY.

Franco shouted, "Ay caramba! This should not be happening! Who are these people, Mizu?"

Mizu explained, "I go to school with Max Prodigus, Jr., whose parents are very wealthy. When I was getting ready to leave school yesterday, he and his younger brothers were handing out flyers to everyone. It looked as if they were inviting the entire school!"

"#CoolPool," exclaimed Arielle. "That sounds like a blast! I'll need to go shopping for a new swimsuit if we're going to this party. It's been so long since I've been shopping because all this Super Sustainables stuff has been keeping me busy. And there's no way I would be caught wearing the same swimsuit from last year. Birdie, we have to stop at the mall on the way home."

"I thought there was more to life than shopping?" Birdie teased.

Arielle glared at Birdie, suddenly sorry for having shared her experience in the locker room with her yesterday. She had been so mad when she got home and had needed to vent.

"See if I tell you anything again," she threatened. "I was upset and it just came out. Haven't you ever said something accidentally when you were stressed? *Of course* shopping is important!" she emphasized.

Tara glared at her. "She did not just say that! Are you serious? Can't you stop thinking about yourself and your shopping addiction for just one minute and try to process what's going on here?" she demanded.

*Here we go again,* she thought, still not sure whether she was going to have patience for the cheerleader's whimsical notions.

Birdie smiled before commenting. "Finally someone besides me tells her that. Welcome to the club, sister."

"You girls are far too serious," replied Arielle. "It's just a pool party, so let's keep things in perspective."

Tara answered tersely through gritted teeth, feeling her patience dissolve even further. "This is not just a pool party! This flyer says there will be a lot of activities involving water, which means wasting it, not to mention the tons of bad habits they're promoting and encouraging. We're going to have to do something. Mizu's right—this is our first crisis!"

"Okay, alright. Don't get your panties in a bind!" Arielle said, raising her hands. "I guess I was focusing on the pool party part. I'm just a girl, you know, I still like having fun."

Arielle was still finding all of this especially difficult, for she already had her group of friends at school—who were all popular and cool like her. She generally didn't get along with nerdy girls like Tara, and didn't really even give them the time of day. So it felt particularly awkward to be apologizing and explaining herself to someone like that. It was clear by now that Arielle and Tara were polar opposites, and everyone knew it was going to take a lot of effort from each of them to put their differences aside and try to work together for a common goal. Now that they were both part of the same team, they *had* to make this work.

"Hey, chill out, *chicas*," said Franco as he stepped between the girls. "You're both right, and maybe this party can be a good thing for us," he continued, his brain starting to kick into gear with a plan.

"How can this be good, Franco?" asked Tara, still a little frazzled from yet another tiff with Arielle. She was a peace-loving girl and really tried to avoid confrontations like that. "This is clearly a complete disaster!"

Franco explained simply. "This is a great opportunity for us to reach a whole bunch of kids at the same time, in one place, with our message about how important it is to save water. I vote we go."

"Hey, that's actually not a bad idea," said Mizu, looking more cheerful.

"Okay, but let's just go as ourselves," said Tara. "Maybe we can talk to everyone and get them to see that what they're doing is wrong."

Arielle agreed, but didn't share her real reasons. After her showdown with Tara, she felt certain they would all judge her for still being a bit unsure about this whole superhero thing. And the last thing she wanted to do was go to a party in a superhero costume, just to be laughed at. *Yeah, I'll just keep that to myself for now,* she thought. *#AGirlsGottaHaveSomeSecrets!*

"Okay, then, it's settled," said Franco. "Let's meet here on Saturday at ten to go to the Prodigus' party and see what it's all about … and if we can make a difference."

The four heroes all nodded in agreement before parting ways.

# The Calm Before the Storm

Chapter 13

# The Party

"#IAmSoHotToday," Arielle complained. "I hate sweating like this. It's so gross!"

It was Saturday morning, the sun was beating down, and the day was sure to be another hot one. The four kids had gathered at the totem pole and were going over their plan for the party.

"Yeah, with it being so hot, I'm sure everyone is going to go to the Prodigus' party to keep cool," Mizu said. "I just hope they'll listen to what we have to say."

"Well," said Tara, practical as usual, "let's get going. The sooner we get there, the more water we will be able to save."

"Have you all got your SustainaWatches, just in case we need our super selves?" Franco asked.

They all nodded and waved their arms to show their watch-covered wrists. Birdie flew overhead and squawked loudly to cheer them on.

"Good luck, team! This is our first adventure together. Let's do it right." Then she flew down and perched on Arielle's shoulder.

"I'm so excited about all of this," Arielle said to Birdie. "And I'm so glad you're here with me. I think it's time," she added with a wink.

"Time for what?" asked Birdie.

"Time for a quick selfie, you know?" replied Arielle, holding the camera phone ready to snap a photo. "Smile. Say 'Girl Power!'" Before Birdie could respond, Arielle snapped a photo.

"You're never going to change, are you?" asked Birdie, smiling at her best friend.

"L-O-L! Not likely!" Arielle said with a grin.

The four unlikely friends set off for the Prodigus estate in silence, absorbed in their own thoughts of what they were about to do.

The gates to the estate had been left open, and the four of them made their way up the long driveway to the front door. On either side of the driveway were lush green lawns with big sprinklers continuously watering them.

"Tsk! Tsk! They're clearly watering more than twice a week," Tara said as she looked at the drought-intolerant landscaping.

They heard shouting and laughter from out back.

"Sounds like things are in full swing here already," Franco commented.

At the door, a tall blonde woman wearing a colorful dress greeted them. She had beautifully styled hair and nails and picture-perfect makeup. "Hello," she said.

"Hi," said Mizu, handing her the flyer. "I go to school with Max Jr. I hope it's okay that I brought some friends with me."

"I'm Mrs. Prodigus, Max Jr.'s mom. And sure that's okay—the more, the merrier. Come on in. Everyone's out back," she said as she welcomed them into the house.

They all thanked her. Arielle paused to have a look at Mrs. Prodigus' fingernails and said, "You're very pretty, Mrs. Prodigus, and I love your nail color. Where did you buy it?"

"Thanks, sweetheart. You can call me Abby," Mrs. Prodigus replied.

Tara looked at Arielle with an astounded expression and said sternly, "You are not here to exchange beauty secrets. Let's go!" She grabbed Arielle's hand and pulled her away. The four of them continued walking through the mansion toward the party in the backyard where they regrouped with Birdie. The young heroes stood with wide-open mouths as they stared in astonishment.

Directly off the patio was the largest pool they had ever seen, complete with an elaborate water slide beside it. At the top, a hose with running water had been attached to each side of the slide to keep it slippery.

"Wow, this party is totally lit!" Franco said, interrupting their state of shock.

"It's what?" asked Mizu as he looked at Franco in confusion.

"Oh come on, *amigo*, that's slang for, it's happening, hopping, raging."

An embarrassed Mizu lowered his head and said softly, "Oh, right."

"Come on, guys, we can finish our slang lesson later," Tara interrupted. "It sounds like most of the commotion is coming from the other side of the pool."

They made their way across the yard, littered with candy wrappers and bags of chips. Tara bent down and started collecting them to throw them away. She looked for a trash bin, but there was none in sight.

"How can there be no trash bins here?" she asked the others. Before they could reply, a hand touched her on the shoulder. She was so startled that she nearly jumped out of her own skin and accidentally dropped the litter she had just picked up.

"Don't worry about picking that up," said a man with a lit cigar dangling between his lips. "We have a cleaning company coming in tomorrow to clean up the mess. Wait a minute—aren't you the girl who scolded me the other day about picking up my litter on the street?"

Tara answered a little sheepishly, "Yes, sir, that was me."

"Well," said Mr. Prodigus, "you're at my house now, so we'll play by my rules. Just go and enjoy yourselves. That's what this party is all about."

"But…" Tara began, but couldn't get any further because Franco tugged her arm and pulled her away.

"Let's see what else we're up against first, Tara," he said.

Birdie flew down toward them and said, "You guys have to come to the other side of the pool to see what's going on there."

They all quickly followed Birdie to have a look. A steep bank descended sharply to a flat, grassy area, where most of the action was happening. One side was lined with thick hedges of bushes and trees which ran alongside the house, bordering a dry, empty field on the other side. Down the middle of the bank, a huge slip-and-slide had been set up, again with a constantly running hose as its water source. Sprinklers gushed water nonstop, with kids playing around in it.

On the same level as the pool, next to the bushes, three big barbecues had been set up. Mr. Prodigus stood there smoking while flipping burgers and grilling hot dogs for the hordes of hungry kids running around his yard. As they watched, he took his cigar out of his mouth, flicked the ash onto the ground, and placed the cigar on the short wall next to the shrubs while he carried on cooking.

Two large hoses were set up at the furthest end of the yard, where teams of boys, each led by one of the twins, were using them in the ultimate water fight. In the middle of the yard sat a huge, water-filled dunking tank with water guns in front of it. Next to it was a filling station where you could refill your water gun, then aim it at the red circle on the tank and fire away. If you hit the target square on, you would dunk your friend. A short distance from the dunking tank was the biggest bouncy castle they had ever seen, and it also had a pool full of bubbles and a long slide. Still another hose provided the water to keep the bouncy castle wet for sliding.

"Oh, my God!" exclaimed Mizu. "It's worse than I imagined. Just look at all this water being wasted!"

"Look what's happening to the bank where the slip-and-slide is," Tara pointed out. With all the water spilling over and young people running up and down the bank, the grass was getting churned up and the dirt beneath was beginning to erode. "Imagine if they do that all day," she said to the others. "No bank will be left!"

"What are all those colored things on the ground?" Arielle asked. "More litter?"

"I'm not sure," Franco replied.

As they stood there taking it all in, they saw kids filling up water balloons with the garden hose—which was running continually—and flinging them at each other with screams of delight. As the balloons burst, pieces of latex littered the ground like colorful confetti.

"That is so bad for the environment," Tara exclaimed with a stomp of her foot. "Don't they know that latex isn't biodegradable, and will damage our earth? Not to mention that if animals try to eat it, thinking it's food, they'll choke!"

Facing the Drought

The Party

"Right," said Mizu. "It's time for action. What are we going to do?"

"Mmmmmm, let's cut them off at the source," Franco said. "We'll each take a hose and turn it off. Meet back here on top of the bank, and hopefully we can get everyone to listen to us."

Off they went to turn off the hoses. They gathered on top of the bank to wait for the partygoers to realize what had happened. It didn't take long before there were shouts of "Hey, what happened to the water?"

Mr. Prodigus, eager to restore the party, shouted that he would sort it out. But as he started to walk past them, Franco, Mizu, Tara, and Arielle blocked his path. Mizu, their representative for the element of water, stepped forward to speak.

"Sir," he said, "there's so much water being wasted at this party. We're in the middle of an extreme drought, and nobody knows when it's going to end. We have to conserve our water before it all runs out. Please, sir, put a stop to this."

Mr. Prodigus looked completely startled. With no attempt at hiding his growing anger, he said, "I beg your pardon! This is *my* house, and what I do here is my business!"

"That's where you're wrong, sir," Mizu continued. "We are *all* responsible, and we all have to do our part to help."

"Well, I never!" said Mr. Prodigus. "We're all just having a little fun on a hot day. This is my house and I say we can do what we want. You didn't have to come here—and if you don't like it, you can leave!"

By now, some of the other party-goers had gathered to see what was going on. They began jeering and mocking Mizu.

"What a nerd."

"Go home, then!"

"That's the weird kid from my class."

"Why did you bother coming?"

"You're ruining our party, man!"

"But you have to listen to me," Mizu said, but he could hardly hear himself over the chorus of boos, hisses, and shouting.

Franco stepped in and tried to help. "He's right!" he shouted. "You guys have to listen before it's too late."

It was no use. Nobody seemed to care about what Mizu was saying. They just wanted to have fun and enjoy themselves. Finally, Mr. Prodigus held up his hands and told the kids to keep quiet so he could speak.

"We're not causing any harm to anybody else, and we're having a party here. Now I'm going to turn the water back on and if you guys have such a problem with it, you're welcome to leave. I'm not going to stand here and be told what to do by a bunch of know-it-all teenagers!" With that, he marched off.

Max Jr. turned to Mizu. "Why do you want to ruin our party?"

"I don't want to ruin your party," Mizu replied, desperate to get them to understand. "I'm trying to tell you how wasteful it is. You can still have a party without wasting water."

"You're just a big party pooper!" Rudy said. "I think you and your nerdy friends should leave now!"

"Excuse me! Do I look like a nerdy girl to you, little monkey?" Arielle interrupted, unable to contain herself any longer.

Before Rudy could reply, shouts and snickering erupted as water started gushing all over the yard again. The kids all ran back to resume their activities.

The four friends stood there, dejected. They had tried, but failed on their very first mission!

Feeling totally despondent, they stood watching all the water running freely around the yard again, wondering what to do now. They were starting to realize just how hard it was going to be to get people to listen to them.

Suddenly there was an ear-splitting screech from Arielle. Tara clamped her hands over her ears and gave Arielle a look of pure annoyance. "Why are you screaming…?" But the rest of her question was drowned out and she started screaming too. They were being pelted from above with water balloons!

"What the—" Franco shouted.

"Who's doing this?" shouted Mizu as he put his hands up to protect his head.

"Go home, losers!" came a shout from up high, followed by lots of laughter.

"Yeah, get out of here!" others shouted at them as the onslaught of balloons continued.

Most of the guests stopped what they were doing to watch the four heroes driven humiliatingly from the party. Even Mr. Prodigus was laughing. *What a way to teach your kids how to treat others,* Tara thought angrily.

As the four heroes ran for the house to take cover, Tara noticed that some kids had climbed up onto the roof and were throwing the water balloons down from there.

"How did they get up there?" she shouted to the others. "It's a three-story mansion!"

"Who cares?" Arielle shouted back. "They've totally ruined my hair! It's all wet!"

They got to the door of the mansion and each grabbed a towel from a big pile to dry themselves off.

"Come on, guys," said Franco. "Let's get out of here. We need a new plan."

"Yeah," agreed Tara. "This is going to be harder than I thought. I mean how are we supposed to educate people, if nobody will even listen to us?"

"I think we should go back to the totem pole and summon Mother Nature for help," Franco suggested. "Maybe she can tell us what we have to do to get people to listen to us."

They made their way through the mansion to the front of the house and began chattering among themselves as they walked back down the long driveway. Arielle, Franco, and Tara were so busy trying to decide what to do next that they didn't realize Mizu was no longer with them. When they were about halfway down the driveway, Birdie flew over to them and said, "Hey guys, what's wrong with Mizu?"

They looked around and saw him sitting by himself on the steps in front of the house, looking sad and depressed.

"Hey, Mizu, is everything okay, *amigo?*" asked Franco as he ran toward him.

"What happened?" asked Tara.

"I'm sorry I brought you here," said Mizu. "This is all my fault. I brought you to this party and now everyone thinks you guys are weird like me. Maybe Mother Nature chose the wrong kid for this mission. I don't have the personality for it because nobody likes me, nobody respects me, and nobody listens to me. I don't feel like I'm a good fit for the Super Sustainables...and if I stay, I'm just going to bring the rest of you down. You'll have a better chance of succeeding on this mission if it's just the three of you," he finished, hanging his head.

Arielle, Franco, and Tara looked at Mizu, not sure what to do. They still didn't know each other all that well yet, and it was clear that Mizu needed someone who would say the right things. Arielle nudged Tara with her elbow and Tara looked at her, trying to understand what she was getting at.

Then she noticed that Arielle was making her eyes wide and inching her head slightly in Mizu's direction as if she was telling her to go to him. Tara mouthed "Me?" to Arielle.

Arielle nodded encouragingly.

Arielle might have been an airhead cheerleader, but she knew people and could read body language like a pro. She had noticed how shyly Mizu had watched Tara when they met at the totem pole, and knew that Mizu kind of liked her. She hadn't said anything because she knew how embarrassed Mizu would have been, and Tara hadn't really stopped biting her head off since they first met. So she had kept this insight to herself. *What he sees in her is anyone's guess,* Arielle thought. *But if anyone is going to get through to him now, it's Tara!*

Tara sat down next to Mizu. "Mizu, you're not alone in this. We're all in this together, just as Mother Nature intended. It's not your fault that you brought us here and nobody listened. They didn't only ignore you—they ignored all of us. You did the right thing by telling us about the party because we had to at least *try* to stop it. Mother Nature chose you because you care deeply about the earth and want to save it. I know how it feels when people don't take you seriously, and laugh and make fun of you for trying to do the right thing, because people don't listen to me either. I know what it's like to be different. But now, being different means something else—it means we're special because we got chosen for this mission. And now we have to stand together and be strong and help one another so we can make a difference."

She looked up after her speech to find Franco staring at her, and shot him a meaningful look to indicate he should say something, too.

"That's right, *amigo*, you're not alone now. We're all here for you," Franco said, looking over at Arielle. "Right, Arielle?"

"Oh, yes, me too," said Arielle, who had completely zoned out during Tara's speech and was staring off into space while playing with her hair. Both Franco and Tara glared angrily at her, which snapped her back into focus. "I mean, yes, we are all here together, and Birdie too," she said.

Mizu raised his head and looked at Tara, and then at Franco and Arielle. "Thanks, guys, it means a lot to have you as my friends through all of this. This is all so new for me. But it's also very important and exciting," he said as he stood up and smiled to show them that he was feeling better.

"Good to hear, Mizu, now let's get out of here. We need to think of a plan B," said Birdie as she flew loops over their heads.

Chapter 14

# Disaster Strikes

They had just gotten to the bottom of the driveway and were making their way back down the street when a huge gust of wind nearly knocked them over.

"Aww," said Arielle. "My hair!"

Tara rolled her eyes and sighed. "*Again* with your hair, Arielle? We have bigger worries than that, you know."

Birdie jumped in with a laugh. "Hey, Arielle, maybe now's a good time for a selfie!"

Arielle shot both of them a look of annoyance and said, "#Whatever. Very funny, ha!" She was about to give Birdie a playful swat when she saw the look on her face and paused, her hand raised in mid-air. "Birdie, what is it?"

Birdie had begun jumping around on Arielle's shoulder, really agitated. "Seriously, what's wrong, Birdie?"

"I don't know," she replied. "I've just got a bad feeling."

"Yeah, we all do," Mizu said.

Suddenly, Birdie shot off down the street, back toward the Prodigus estate. "Hey, Birdie! Come back here!" Arielle called after her. "I wonder what's gotten into her?" she muttered.

"Should we go after her?" Franco asked, but before Arielle could reply Birdie zoomed back toward them.

"Quick, guys, you have to hurry," she squawked. "There's trouble at the party!"

"What's wrong?" Arielle asked. "After the way we were told to leave, I doubt they want our help."

"No, you don't understand, they need the Super Sustainables—and fast! You have to activate your powers, like *now!* Before it's too late!"

The young heroes looked at one another. This was it. Their very first disaster—besides the party itself, that is. Arielle thought to herself, *#ShowTime!*

And then…no one moved.

Birdie let out a loud squawk. "What are you guys just standing there for? This is an emergency! Hurry up!"

Franco flipped open his SustainaWatch and tapped his fire app. As it opened, releasing the energy of his element, a deep red glow surrounded him. The others stood and watched in stunned amazement as his clothing changed and his shield appeared. His hair became a brighter red and burst up out of his head like a flame. His red outfit had orange flames all over it and he was wearing a pair of golden boots that wound around his legs like flames on his feet.

He looked down at himself and smiled, because at that moment he knew he was Fuego and ready for whatever lay ahead!

"Wow! Totally cool, Arielle! You did a great job with my costume."

"Yeah? I'm glad you like it."

"Come on guys, now it's your turn," he said to the others.

Birdie could not wait to see Tara's transformation. But she looked at Arielle and saw that she was looking more than a little nervous. She flew to her and sat on her shoulders. "Relax, Arielle, it will all be fine."

Tara tapped her own symbol.

The energy of the earth surrounded her in a deep green glow. Arielle crossed her fingers and held her breath, silently repeating the mantra, *Please like it, please like it.* She nervously peeped out of one eye and watched as Tara's clothing changed to green, with the tree-branch pattern snaking over her body. Tara's flip-flops became a pair of brown, gladiator-style sandals. Tara was startled when a long, flower-shaped staff appeared in her hand, and she wondered why both Mizu and Franco's eyes had gotten so wide as she felt a headband appear on her head, sweeping her unruly (now green) hair back off her face.

Birdie looked at Arielle and whispered, "You're right, her hair totally looks like a tree. But to be honest, it suits her. So promise me that you'll never stop believing in yourself as a designer."

"I know, you're right. I have to admit that I totally got cold feet, but I promise it won't happen again," responded Arielle. "Thanks for believing in me," she added with a smile.

Birdie was the first to compliment Tara. "You look great!"

Franco and Mizu were still staring. "Wow, you look so different, Tara," Franco finally said. "So powerful—like a force to be reckoned with."

Arielle grabbed a mirror compact from her backpack and held it up for Tara. "I've been so stressed about how you were going to feel about green hair," she said. "But I hope you like it because you look stunning!"

Tara stared at her reflection for a few seconds, taking in the transformation. It was far removed from what she would have chosen for herself, and definitely different from her usual look. But she had to admit she looked good—and what was more, for the first time in her life, she actually felt pretty.

"Wow! I love it, Arielle. So nice!" she said. "Now I understand why you've been asking me questions about my hair," she added with a slight giggle.

Arielle breathed an audible sigh of relief and gave Tara a smile. "I can honestly say, Tara, you look like the Queen of the Earth."

"Now you can call me Terra," Tara replied, thrilled with her new superhero look.

Mizu stepped forward next, relieved that the SustainaWatches were working exactly as he had intended. He tapped his app, excited to see how he would be transformed. Within seconds, the power of water surrounded him in a turquoise glow and his clothes changed to a blue wetsuit with waves all over and fins on the arms. The wool hat he liked to wear changed to a special snorkel hat, and he had a pair of blue boots with fins to match on his feet. Mizu looked down and liked what he saw.

Disaster Strikes

*Wow, I look so different,* he thought. *Less nerdy and way cooler. I like it!*

"Thanks, Arielle. I really love my new look."

"Glad you like it. You look awesome."

Arielle looked at the others and was so pleased with her designs. The outfits looked even better than she'd imagined they would, and her friends seemed genuinely happy with their superhero fashions.

Now it was her turn. She tapped her air app. A purple glow surrounded her as she became one with the wind and felt her clothes change.

She was wearing a purple mini-skirt and purple knee-high boots with golden swirls at the top. Attached to her shoulders was a yellow cape that flowed out behind her, and she felt her headband wrap itself around her head. She twisted this way and that, trying to get a better look with her compact.

*Where's a full-length mirror when you need one?* she thought. She just came right out and asked the question she was dying to ask.

"How do I look, guys?"

Birdie stifled a giggle. She knew Arielle so well, and wanted to mess with her and say something sarcastic. But she thought this was probably not the time to push Arielle's buttons. "You look great, Arielle, and you know it!"

Arielle smiled, feeling very pleased with herself. "You know what we need to do, guys?" she asked.

Before anyone had a chance to answer her, Birdie piped up, "No, Arielle, this is not the time for a selfie!"

"Hey!" shouted Arielle. "How did you know that's what I was going to say?"

"Because I know you better than you think!"

"Okay, okay. I know there is no time now, but you have to admit this would be #TheSelfieOfTheDay!"

"So shall we go?" Terra asked.

Mizu adjusted his snorkel hat to fit more comfortably and looked at the others with a grin. "Ready for action!" he said.

"*Vámonos* Super Sustainables!" shouted Fuego.

"Hey, guys, wait for me!" shouted Birdie as she began to spin around. She spun so quickly that she looked like a red cyclone. Just when they thought she would surely faint from dizziness, there was a loud cawing noise as she morphed into a tough-looking and larger-than-life California condor.

"You guys aren't the only ones with superpowers!" she told them with an indignant fluff of her feathers. "*Now* we can go!"

"Holy Birdie!" Arielle said, excited and shocked at this unexpected surprise. Birdie had just been a little stuffed toy a few weeks ago, and now she was the largest of all birds. The other heroes were also impressed to see the dramatic change.

# Disaster Strikes

"Close your mouths," Birdie said with a laugh. "We have some people to save! Now, who needs a ride?"

Mizu and Terra shouted in excitement at the same time, "I do!" Both jumped on Birdie's back.

Arielle was about to join them when she felt a strange movement on her back and twisted her head around to see. Her cape stood out straight and flat behind her. It began to flap up and down, almost like a pair of wings.

"*#IAmFlying!*" she screamed. "Humph, I guess not," she added when she didn't immediately take off. She closed her eyes and thought back to that day in the gym and the time at Mizu's house where she had briefly flown with the wind beneath her. She used those memories to imagine how to take off. This was her first *official* time, after all. As the cape began flapping faster, she pictured herself floating in the air. Suddenly she was lifted off the ground.

*Oh, what the heck!* she thought, and gave it her all.

Before she knew it, she was flying high above the clouds. She flew through the air, looping and twisting as she went. She landed next to Birdie and said, "All right, I'm ready to go now."

"All about you, as usual," Birdie muttered. "This is not the Arielle Show, you know!"

"Yeah, yeah," Arielle said with a grin. She was far too excited about being able to really fly to be annoyed by Birdie's snarky comments.

They all looked at Fuego, and Birdie asked, "You want a lift?"

He started to say yes, but suddenly felt his boots getting hot. Two little flames shot out the back of each one like rocket thrusters. "Way cool!" he said with a grin. "I'm good, but thanks anyway, Birdie."

**Disaster Strikes**

They all began making their way back toward the Prodigus estate, but Arielle—wanting to try out her new flying cape—decided to zoom ahead. She was waiting at the gates to report to the others what had happened.

"It's bad!" she told them. "When the wind picked up just as we were leaving, it must have blown Mr. Prodigus' cigar into the dry bushes. I noticed earlier that he carelessly set it down on the wall while he was grilling the burgers. In this hot, dry weather, the bushes caught fire. I guess even though there was water all around, it was only in the other side of the backyard and never got to the drier parts near the grills. Now everyone is running around and screaming, and in the chaos, two grills were knocked over—and with this wind, the flames are rushing toward the house. Some of the young people are trapped in the yard and panicking because the bank became so wet and muddy that they just keep sliding back down when they try to climb up. We have to do something before someone gets hurt!"

"Why don't they just use the hoses to put out the fire?" Terra asked.

"They're all down in the far end of the yard, and aren't long enough to reach," Arielle said. "And the ones by the pool are attached to the slide so they're absolutely no help. Mrs. Prodigus is running around screaming that all her precious things are going to burn and Mr. Prodigus is trying to put the fire out by throwing glasses of water at it, but it's already way too big for that to work."

"Okay then," Fuego said. "Arielle, you have to get the wind to calm down so the fire doesn't spread, and I'll stop the flames. Terra, try to get the landslide under control and Mizu—"

"I'll find a way to use the water to extinguish the fire," Mizu finished.

As the Super Sustainables ran through the house to the backyard, they couldn't believe what they were seeing. The boys were running around, not quite sure where to go, and many of the girls were crying. But nobody seemed to be doing anything useful.

"Right, guys," Fuego said, taking charge. "Let's do this."

"Do what?" Mizu said. "We know what we're *supposed* to do, but we've never used our powers before. I don't know how to control them."

"Yeah," agreed Arielle. "How will we know what to do?"

"Mother Nature wouldn't have sent us if we weren't ready," Fuego said confidently.

"But Fuego," Mizu replied, looking very pale, "*she* didn't send us here. *I* told you about the party. Mother Nature doesn't know we're here at all."

"Oh," replied Fuego, as though this thought had just occurred to him. "Right. Umm…"

They had never been the Super Sustainables before, and hadn't ever used their powers. Now they faced an emergency, with no instruction manual handy. How would they know exactly what to do?

"Well," said Terra, "we're here now and there's clearly trouble. We have to at least try. I'm sure we won't make things any worse."

"Right, so Arielle, you and I are up first," Fuego said. "Let's go."

Arielle rubbed the swirl on her headband vigorously and repeated the words, "Calm, wind," over and over.

Fuego jumped into action. He ran at the flames, held up his shield, and silently commanded them to stop in their tracks.

"Arielle," Terra cried out. "The wind is picking up! What are you doing?"

"I don't know!" Arielle said, a frantic expression on her face. "I'm trying as hard as I can." She scrunched up her face in concentration and rubbed the tornado symbol even harder. *Come on!* she willed the wind.

Mizu and Terra watched in horror as Fuego ran at the flames with his shield. The flames rebounded off the shield and shot up into the air, where they got picked up by the strong wind Arielle was creating. Within seconds they were carried over to a large tree next to the house. The tree ignited and quickly became a roaring blaze.

"*Stop!*" yelled Terra and Mizu.

"You're making it worse!" screeched Terra.

Arielle immediately stopped rubbing her headband, but the damage was done—a new fire had been started. Mr. Prodigus stared at them with a dumbfounded expression. "Who are you?" he shouted. "Are you trying to burn down my house?"

Fuego looked at them, sweat pouring down his face from the heat of the flames and the effort of holding them at bay. The flames had formed a sort of arc between the ground and his shield and were bouncing off him. "I don't know how much longer I can hold back these flames," he said through gritted teeth. "You guys have to do something, and fast. If I let go, the house is a goner for sure."

"I'm so sorry!" Arielle wailed, looking close to tears. "I obviously didn't mean to do that."

"No time for self-pity now," Terra snapped. "We need a plan. Just give me a moment to think."

But the next moment they heard panicked screams. They looked around, trying to find the source.

Suddenly Arielle clutched Terra's arm and felt her knees buckle under her. "#OHMYGOD!"

Chapter 15

The Power of Four

"What?" Terra demanded. "What now? I don't have time for your melodrama, Arielle. I'm trying to think of a plan to fix your mess!"

"Look!" The word came out in a strangled cry as Arielle pointed upwards.

Terra followed her gaze and felt her blood run cold. She grabbed Mizu by the arm and pointed. His mouth fell open in shock.

The kids who had been pelting them with water balloons earlier were trapped on the roof. Arielle suddenly realized they must have climbed up the big tree next to the house to get onto the roof earlier— the same tree now burning because of her error.

In the few seconds it took them to absorb what they were seeing, the flames began licking at the gutters on the roof. The boys trapped up there were starting to panic. They were on a small section of roof with a gentle gradient. There wasn't really anywhere to move to get away from the flames, as the rest of the roof was far too steep. If they tried to climb on it, they were sure to slip and fall. They were too high up to safely jump.

"Guuuuys!" shouted Fuego. "A little help here, please."

Terra was the first to gather her composure. "Arielle," she said, "if rubbing your headband fast caused more wind, maybe you should try rubbing it slowly to get the wind to stop?"

"I'm not doing anything else," a shaken Arielle declared. "Count me out. I've done enough damage."

Terra noticed that she was pale, flustered, and looked terrified. She took Arielle by the hand and looked her in the eye. "No!" she declared sternly. "We are a team and we need you! No matter what we do, we won't be able to solve this without your help. While the wind is blowing, the fire will keep spreading. Arielle, you can do this. I believe in you."

"Me too," Mizu said.

Arielle didn't look convinced. She looked up at the kids stuck on the roof, who were now crying hysterically, at Fuego, fighting the flames alone, and then back to Terra. Her eyes filled with tears and every inch of her was shaking.

Then, as Arielle was taking in the scene of destruction before her, there was a loud crash. The gutter had fallen and the flames had caught hold of the roof. If they didn't do something soon, the house would burn and the boys on the roof would be seriously hurt—or worse, killed.

"Arielle, we can't waste any more time. Mother Nature chose you for a reason. I know this is scary, but we can do this together. Keep your eyes on me and rub your headband slowly. Please, just try!" Terra pleaded.

As tears started to stream down Arielle's cheeks, she grabbed Terra's hand and squeezed it tightly, then scrunched up her eyes, lifted her right hand, and began to rub the cyclone symbol in a slow, stroking rhythm.

As she connected with her element, she felt the wind begin to calm until she couldn't feel even the slightest breeze against her skin.

"You did it!" Terra shouted.

Arielle opened her eyes and realized she had got it right. She wiped her eyes determinedly and looked at Terra. "Thanks for your help. I really needed that," she said. "Now let's go save these kids. *Birdie!*" she shouted.

Birdie swooped down from the sky and landed in front of her. "What can I do?" she asked.

"Do you think your beak is strong enough to break through whatever is binding those hoses to the slides by the pool? If we can get at least one of them free, it might just be long enough to put out the fire on the roof so we can rescue the boys."

"I'll try," Birdie said, and flew off.

Mizu, Terra, and Arielle waited with bated breath as they watched Birdie struggle to get the hose free. Her beak was really strong, but there was a real danger that, as the hose was tightly bound to the slide, she might puncture it — and then it would be useless.

Their worry was for nothing, because a few moments later the hose was free. Mizu ran over, picked it up, and aimed it at the flames, but it was too short. He tried angling the hose in different ways to get the water to follow a different trajectory. But whichever way he tried, the stream of water fell just short.

"Seriously!" Arielle shrieked, stomping her foot. "Can we not catch a break here?"

"Let me try from higher up," Birdie suggested. She picked up the hose in her beak and flew as high as she could with it, then aimed it at the fire. But the water still wouldn't reach.

Arielle looked up at the boys on the roof. The flames were spreading quickly and they had all inched to the edge of the roof as far from the flames as they could. One of them was starting to panic and scrambled over to a steeper part of the roof.

"Oh no!" Arielle said. "If he climbs up there he's sure to fall."

She shouted up to him to stay put, but the boy wasn't listening. Suddenly, it was clear to Arielle what she had to do. She instinctively kicked off from the ground and flew up onto the roof to keep the boys calm while the others figured out a plan. As she approached the roof, the boy took a flying leap and tried to grab one of the tiles on the roof. But it was wet with water from the water balloons, and his hands were slippery. He couldn't hold on. He slipped and slid down the roof, screaming the whole way.

Arielle landed on the roof just in time to grab him by the hand as he slipped over the edge. She hung on for dear life as the boy dangled dangerously.

Mizu and Terra stood frozen, watching in horror. Arielle wasn't strong enough to hold on for long, and if the boy fell, he'd surely get hurt.

Fuego, watching the events unfold as he battled the flames, was suddenly struck with an idea and shouted, "Birdie! Go and help. Put those boys on your back and fly them down to the ground."

Mizu slapped his forehead in frustration. *Well obviously!* he chided himself. He looked at Terra as it all became clear. "We're thinking like normal kids," he told her. "That's the problem. We need to think like superheroes, and for superheroes, nothing is impossible!"

They watched Birdie swoop majestically up and hover under the boy hanging from the roof. "It's okay, you can let go now, Arielle. I've got him."

Arielle saw that the boys were frightened to see such a large bird. "Don't worry, guys, Birdie's here to help us out," she reassured them.

Birdie caught the boy as he fell, then glided safely to the ground, set him down, and zipped up to the roof to get the next, and then the next. When all the boys were safe, Arielle did a graceful backflip off the roof and landed daintily next to Mizu.

"Okay, so what did I hear you say the plan is?" she asked.

"We've got to stop thinking like regular kids," he told her. "We have to think big now, if we're going to figure this out. Mother Nature gave us powers and we're clever kids. We can get this situation under control. Arielle, you did a great job saving those kids."

Mizu turned to Terra. "Now it's your turn. You are Terra. Go stop that landslide and get the kids at the bottom of the lawn to safety while I figure out how to help Fuego put out this fire."

"Got it!" Terra said with a smile. She knew he was right. It was their first disaster and there had been a few hiccups. Now that they were thinking like heroes with a plan, there was a new level of confidence among them that they could overcome these challenges.

For the first time that day, she felt as if they really could do it. She ran to the top of the steep bank and watched as the young people scrambled around, trying to climb up. As they slipped and slid back down, uprooting more and more earth, she realized she needed to act fast. She held out her staff and a green glow surrounded the bulb at the top. She pointed it toward the earth and shouted, "Stop!"

The mini-landslide ceased. She pointed her staff to the farthest part of the garden, a spot against the hedges where it wasn't a complete mudslide, and carved a path into the earth for the kids to walk up.

"It's safe to climb up now," she told the ones stuck at the bottom of the hill.

They stared at her in amazement as they made their way to safety. She heard a few people whisper, "Who is that?" and she could only smile.

Now it was up to Mizu to save the day. The flames on the ground were becoming too strong for Fuego. They had already pushed him a couple of feet closer to the house. The roof was engulfed with flames where the boys had been just a few minutes before, and Mizu knew he had to do something spectacular before Fuego lost the fight and the whole house caught fire. He quickly scanned the scene for inspiration, then closed his eyes for a second to gather his thoughts. He stood closer to Fuego so that the flames were on one side of him and the pool on the other.

"Hey, *amigo*, you got a plan yet?" Fuego asked. He was drenched in sweat and breathless from exertion.

"Oh yeah!" Mizu replied with a grin.

He picked up the snorkel attached to his hat and pointed it at the pool. He closed his eyes and thought of the perfect wave, just as he had at the beach that day. Then he opened his eyes and flicked the end of the snorkel in the direction of the fire. Miraculously, the water rose up out of the pool and formed the arc of a wave before crashing down over the flames on the ground and in the tree, completely dousing them.

"Whoa, dude!" said Fuego, drenched from the wave. "That was awesome!" He came over, dripping wet, to high-five Mizu, who returned it with a big grin.

"Thank you," Fuego said. "I couldn't have held on for much longer. Those flames were so strong and kept pushing me further and further back. Guess I'm going to have to start pumping some iron at the gym!"

"We're not done yet," Mizu added. "We still have to put out the fire on the roof but the hoses are all too short. I have a plan, and I'm going to need you all to help me. Where are the girls?"

"We're here," squealed Arielle. "That was amazing, Mizu!"

Mizu blushed in response. "Where's Birdie?" he asked to divert the attention away from himself.

"I'm here," she answered as she swooped down from the sky.

"Can you detach the other three hoses from the slides?"

"Can a fish swim?" she said with a wink, and flew off.

When all of the hoses were freed up, Mizu told each of his friends to grab one and point it at the house.

"But we tried this already," Arielle said. "They're too short."

Mizu laughed. He had come into his own today and was on a roll. "Yes, they were too short when we were trying to put out the fire like regular kids. But I've got this." He wiggled his snorkel hat around. "If we work together now and use my power, that fire will be out in a few minutes and the Prodigus estate will be saved."

"Okay, let's do it!" they all agreed, and aimed their hoses at the house. Just as before, the stream of water was too short. But this time Mizu aimed his snorkel hat at the water, closed his eyes, and scrunched his brow in concentration. He flicked the snorkel hat toward the house, just as he had before when he was creating the wave, expecting the same result.

"Mizu, dude," Fuego said. "Nothing's happening!"

"What?" said Mizu, opening his eyes and seeing that the water still wasn't reaching the roof, which was still ablaze.

"I don't understand. This is what I did earlier and it worked. How come it isn't working now?"

"You created that wave from a big body of water," Terra suggested. "These are just small garden hoses. Maybe it works differently?"

"AAAARGH!" shouted Arielle in frustration. "Could Mother Nature not have just given us an instruction manual to study? How are we supposed to figure this all out on our own?"

"*Amigo*," Fuego said, "go to the pool and make a wave like before. Just make a bigger one so it will reach all the way to the house."

"I can't," wailed Mizu in despair. "The pool is empty from the last wave."

At that moment, Mrs. Prodigus came running out of the house screaming hysterically. "All my things! Everything will be burned! The house is burning down! *Max,* you have to do something!"

They looked to Mr. Prodigus, who was standing rooted to the spot, clearly frozen in fear.

"Well, he isn't going to be any help, is he?" Terra said sarcastically.

Then Birdie came up with an idea. "You need a bigger body of water. Right, Mizu?"

"Yeah.

"Ok, so what if we all stand and hold the hoses together, so the four streams of water become one?" she suggested.

"Four become one!" Mizu agreed.

They held the hoses together and Mizu tried again. Joining them together helped the water reach the roof, but only a small area of the flames could be doused. The fire had already spread beyond the reach of the water.

Mizu looked defeated, but just as he was about to throw in the towel, Arielle jumped up and shouted. "Here, Fuego, hold my hose. And Mizu, do that again."

"What? Why?" he asked. "It's not working."

"Just do it, all right?"

He agreed because at this point, what did they have to lose by trying?

He summoned all his power and went for one final thrust with his snorkel, willing the water to travel further and be stronger to put out the flames.

As Mizu propelled the water forward, they all felt another force from behind. It was Arielle. She was creating a strong gust of wind to push the water further forward to reach the whole area of the roof.

"It's working!" Fuego shouted excitedly. "You guys are doing it!"

Mizu's face was showing the strain of holding the water steady for an extended period of time, while Arielle's brow was furrowed in a way that Birdie had only ever seen before when she tackled her algebra homework.

Both struggled to hold on, but neither gave up until all the flames had been doused.

"That's it!" screamed Terra after what seemed like hours, when in fact it had only been minutes. "It's out! You guys did it!"

A cheer erupted from all the partygoers as the Super Sustainables all high-fived and hugged one another in relief.

"Great thinking, Arielle," Mizu said.

"It was nothing, Mizu," Arielle conceded graciously. "You were the star here today!"

"Yeah," Terra agreed. "You were fantastic, Mizu."

"I couldn't have done it without you guys," Mizu said as he blushed.

"But the big question remains," said a voice. "Who are you guys?" It was Max Jr.

Fuego stepped forward. "We are the Super Sustainables," he said. "We represent the earth and we came here to prevent this from becoming a huge disaster."

Mr. Prodigus and the twins came forward to stand with Max Jr. "You represent who?" Mr. Prodigus asked as if he had just heard a joke.

"The earth. We are its voice," added Mizu, repeating what Fuego just said. "The earth is getting damaged beyond repair by human behavior. So we're here to prevent problems like the one that happened here today, and show you how to be more careful with the earth's precious resources."

"You guys are not the first to tell us that today," Mr. Prodigus said, folding his arms defensively. "But I still don't know where you all get off coming into my house and telling me what to do. I actually had things under control and don't really appreciate you all bursting in here and interfering!"

"Actually, sir," said Fuego, "if we hadn't arrived when we did, your house and everything in it would have completely gone up in flames, and people could have been seriously hurt."

"Oh, nonsense!" Mr. Prodigus said, putting his hands on his hips. Now that the danger was over, Mr. Prodigus was back to his usual cocky, arrogant self. "It was just a little fire. I'd have had it out in a few minutes without all these theatrics if you had just left it to me. Besides, I called the fire department—they should be here any minute."

Fuego turned to the crowd that had gathered. "We're in a drought and the land is really dry. That means the tiniest spark can cause a huge fire. Fire safety is especially important during a drought. What if there's not enough water to put out a fire? Then it becomes a threat to humans, animals, your homes, as well as the trees and plants."

"You're making a mountain out of a molehill, young man," Mr. Prodigus said with a huff.

"No, he's right," Arielle said. "I'll bet you don't even know what happened. Everything was fine until there was a bit of wind, then one tiny spark—from the cigar *you* left unattended—caused a raging fire because everything is so dry. The shrubs caught fire quickly, and the wind helped it spread even faster."

Mr. Prodigus gave an uncomfortable "harrumph" and adjusted his belt. He did not like being made to look like a fool in front of all these people. At that moment, though, a loud sobbing noise came from inside the house. Clearly Mrs. Prodigus was still very upset at the day's turn of events.

"You kids are a bunch of know-it-alls," Mr. Prodigus said, pointing his finger at the four superheroes. "And I think it's very inappropriate, not to mention rude, to come in here trying to tell me what I should and shouldn't do. Don't you know who I am? I told you things were under control and I don't want to hear another word about it. Now, I'm going to see if my wife is all right, and when I come back I expect to find you off my property!" He turned on his heel and stomped into the house.

Max Jr. made a move to follow his dad but then seemed to think again. With a grumpy scowl he shoved his hands in his pockets and looked down at the ground, and stayed where he was.

Lance and Rudy had all but forgotten their fear from the fire. Getting to meet real superheroes face-to-face had made them far too excited to feel anxious.

Lance stepped closer to where the Super Sustainables were standing and asked them in a whisper, "Are you guys for real?"

Rudy joined his brother, adding, "Is all you said really true?"

Terra smiled and replied kindly, "Yes, it's all true. We all have to start doing our part and working together. That way, all of you can be heroes, too."

An angry, booming voice interrupted Terra. Mr. Prodigus was shouting from inside the house. "Boys! Come inside, now! I don't want these weird 'heroes' filling your heads with more nonsense! They call themselves the Super Sustainables but it's more like Super Silliness, if you ask me!"

Mr. Prodigus continued to rant and rave from inside and Max Jr., Lance, and Rudy looked very uncomfortable. They clearly wanted to stay and listen but knew they had better obey their father, as he was hopping mad.

Max Jr. spoke up. "We'd better go, guys, before Dad really loses it."

"Yeah," agreed Lance and Rudy. They started to make their way inside the house. Suddenly Rudy turned back, grabbed one of the party flyers littering the yard, and asked with a huge grin, "Can I get your autographs?" Standing behind his twin brother, Lance did the same.

Arielle stepped forward. "Anyone got a pen?" she asked, grinning proudly.

Before anyone could answer, a loud, booming, angry voice shouted, "Rudy, Lance, get in here *now!*"

The boys nearly jumped out of their skin in fear. They dropped the flyers, turned on their heels, and sprinted into the house.

Arielle was disappointed, as this was the first time she had ever been asked for her autograph. That simple question had made her feel like a real hero.

The Super Sustainables stayed to chat with the kids who were still at the party. Some of them were shocked, scared, and upset by what had just happened, and the heroes were trying to calm everyone down before they left.

One girl stepped forward and asked, "Why do we need to save water? There's water everywhere."

"You're right," said Mizu. "But not all of the water is safe for us to drink. Only a small amount of water on earth is readily drinkable, because the rest is salty."

"Oh, I didn't know that," said the girl. "So it sounds like there isn't enough."

"Unfortunately, no," Mizu answered. He noticed the surprised looks on the faces of the other kids.

"This is why we need to be smart about how we use water," Terra said as she jumped in to support Mizu.

"Can you guys explain to us more about the drought and what we need to do to conserve more water? How can we help the earth like you?" asked another boy, who was listening attentively.

Mizu stepped forward. "Well, a drought basically means that there isn't enough water due to lack of rain and snow, so wasting water like what was happening here today doesn't help an already bad situation."

"And," added Terra, "what most people don't realize is that water affects everything. Too little water can really threaten the environment."

"How?" asked a girl.

Terra thought for a moment before replying. "Well, if there isn't enough rain it doesn't only cause problems for people. Plants and animals also suffer. The plants die and that means the animals won't have anything to eat. Without enough water, it becomes hard for the farmers to grow crops, which means that at some point people might not have enough food to eat, either. People are the only ones who can do something to stop this cycle, and we have to try before it's too late."

"That's right," Arielle said. "When the plants die, there's nothing to hold the soil together anymore, and that means more erosion. When the wind blows, it just makes everything worse and totally changes the way everything looks—kind of like when you have just done your hair and the wind messes it up," she added with a flick of her long blonde hair.

Birdie rolled her eyes. "Only you would use an analogy like that to explain erosion!"

"Hey, whatever works to help people understand," Arielle said with a grin.

"Wow," said a boy who was listening with wide eyes. "I honestly didn't realize everything was so connected."

"Yeah, it really is," said Fuego. "That's why it's so important to try to conserve as much as possible, and encourage others to do the same. Wasting water like you saw here today could mean the next time there's a fire, there might not be enough water to put it out. It could be near your house next time, you never know. Are you prepared to lose your home and all your things for the sake of a fun party?"

Fuego had made his point. As the young people thought about their own homes going up in flames and losing everything, they all looked horrified.

"We really just didn't think," said a girl with dark hair.

"We didn't know it would make all that much difference," another boy added.

"But that's just it," said Mizu. "Every little bit helps. Everything you do is worth something if it saves a little bit of water, because it all adds up. The earth is what we all have in common, and we have to share it with each other, so we need to pay attention to the things we do because our actions affect other people. And like my friends taught me today," he continued, looking at his new friends with a smile, "if we all work together, we can make our earth healthier and happier for all who live here and the generations to come."

"So obviously we won't be having any more water parties," another kid replied sulkily. "But what else can we do to save water?"

"Lots of things," said Mizu. "Like turning off the faucet when you brush your teeth."

Arielle added. "And also, at school in the locker room after gym class, be sure not to leave the faucets and showers running."

"You should actually take shorter showers, instead of baths," continued Mizu. "That will save tons of water. And if there are any leaks in your home, tell your parents to get them repaired right away."

Terra joined the conversation. "Also if you see any sprinklers in your neighborhood running for a long time, or watering the sidewalk or street, you should step up and talk with the homeowner."

"There are lots more ways to conserve water, but the best thing you can do," said Mizu, "is encourage your friends and family to do all these things to conserve water, too. We all need water to live and we don't have an endless supply, so we have to make people see that they have to use water wisely before it's all gone!"

"Now that I think about it," said a boy with blond hair, "my dad uses a hose to wash his car, so I should tell him to use a bucket instead. Right?"

"That's right," said Fuego. "Washing the car with a bucket of water instead of a running hose saves a lot of water."

Another girl stepped up to say, "When I help my mom do the laundry, sometimes I've seen her only put in a few of my cute dresses at a time. So I should tell her to do a full load instead."

"Great idea," said Arielle, thinking of her closet full of cute dresses. "That will save a lot of water, too. And B-T-W, I really like your swimsuit." The girl blushed, feeling special that she was singled out for a compliment from a pretty hero like Arielle.

"Wow, I had no idea there are so many ways to save water," said a boy with brown, curly hair, impressed by all that he had learned. "And if I do these things, can I become a Super Sustainable like you?"

"You sure can," said Terra, smiling back.

"I guess those aren't really big changes, so I can do them. I can pay more attention and be more respectful of the earth," the boy answered.

All the other kids joined in with a loud chorus of, "Me too, me too, me too!"

The Super Sustainables looked at each other and smiled.

"We did it!" said Mizu.

"We sure did," Fuego replied.

"Totally!" said Arielle as she gave Birdie a big hug.

Then suddenly, they heard the sound of a fire truck's siren getting louder as it approached the Prodigus' estate.

Terra said, "I think it's time for us to go now."

As they headed out, she looked around, satisfied, to see some of the guests loading up garbage bags with all the litter.

● ● ● ●

When they got to the bottom of the driveway, Arielle, who could not contain herself any longer because she was so proud of herself, stopped and shouted, "That was, like, so awesome! Like, we absolutely rocked as the Super Sustainables!"

"I'm sure Mother Nature is watching us and smiling with pride," said Terra. "I can just feel it."

Birdie caught up to them, turned back into her smaller self, and landed on Arielle's shoulder. She might have been smaller and cuter, but her tongue was as sharp as ever. "So I was pretty good, right? Nothing like having a tough, fierce California condor on your side when disaster strikes."

Arielle gave Birdie a playful swat and said with a wink at the others, "That's right, Birdie, we couldn't have done it without you."

Then the four of them changed back into their normal clothes by tapping on their apps again.

"It kind of sucks to be normal again, though," Franco commented as they began walking home, back to their ordinary lives.

"Hey, guys. Wait! We forgot to take a selfie together in our cool outfits," Arielle said, disappointed.

"You'll have lots of other opportunities to do that," said Birdie. "I have a feeling we're going to spend a lot of time together, facing many big challenges."

"Oh yeah," Tara agreed. "This is just the beginning..."

Chapter 16

# Blue Turns to Gray

The four heroes gathered at the beach the following day for the Young Surfers Championship. It was a yearly competition where local kids showed off their surfing skills and competed for a scholarship. Mizu had entered several months earlier. He had told the others on the way home from their adventure how nervous he was, so his new friends had promised to come support him and cheer him on.

"No cheating now, *amigo*," Franco said with a laugh. "The others won't stand a chance, anyway. You'd better not create monster waves for yourself."

"Thanks, dude. I won't." Mizu replied as he waxed his surfboard.

Tara sat on her towel, slathering herself with sunblock. She didn't want her skin to burn, and today was another hot one!

Arielle, in her own unique style, was lying stretched out on her towel, soaking up the rays and playing on her phone.

She bolted upright on her towel. "#WhoPostedIt? Hey guys, you'll never believe this!"

Tara sighed. She didn't know if she could handle any more drama.

"What is it?" Mizu asked, looking over at her and squinting in the bright sun.

"We're, like, all over Facebook, Twitter, YouTube, and Instagram. Someone from the party took photos and a video of us in action yesterday as we dealt with the fire and the water, and now everyone is talking about us. The Super Sustainables are trending in a major way!" Arielle held up her phone to show them one of the photos.

Birdie, who had been flying around the beach nearby, landed on the corner of Arielle's towel, glanced at the photo she was showing, and said jokingly, "Really, Arielle? How did you find the time with all that was going on to pose for this photo? Looks like you were working really hard, there."

The Super Sustainables are trending in a major way!

100,000

Arielle, feeling a little embarrassed, answered, "Birdie, do you have to notice *everything?*"

"How can I not notice you when you're taking up half the photo?"

"That's it, Birdie. You've seen enough," said Arielle as she moved the phone out of Birdie's view. "Superheroes need to be ready for action *and* photos at all times."

"Wow, we got 100,000 likes so far. This is awesome!" said Franco, taking Arielle's phone to look more closely. "We might just have a chance to really make a difference at this rate."

He scrolled through the pictures and comments on Arielle's phone. "Wow, I really don't know what to say. It's so cool seeing ourselves online like this, in action—and nobody knows it's us."

"And it's all so positive," Mizu said. "Maybe we actually *do* have a chance to change the world if people will just work with us."

"Yeah," Tara said. "Seems like the word is out about us. Our lives will never be the same again."

As they all chatted about their new "other" life, a loud, booming voice erupted over the public-address system, telling everyone that the competition would soon get underway.

"Well, I guess I'd better get going," Mizu said, and picked up his surfboard.

He was bent over with his back to everyone when he heard Arielle moan, "Hey! Who's in my sun? I can't get an even tan if you block all the rays!"

Franco shouted, "What's that?"

Tara just let out a quiet little, "Oh, no!"

Mizu turned and looked up at the sky. The other heroes stood also, staring wide-eyed. An enormous cloud of thick, black smoke was passing over the beach. They looked at each other in alarm. Mizu turned to Tara and asked, "How can smoke be thick enough to block the sun's rays?"

"Something's not right," she replied. "But where is it coming from?"

They all tried to find the point where it started, but all they could see for miles was a thick, black trail of smoke.

"This is, like, totally not good, right?" Arielle added. "Maybe I should fly up there and take a quick look?"

Tara was about to argue that it probably wasn't a good idea to put herself in danger until they knew what they were dealing with. Before she could get the words out, she spotted something falling from the cloud—heading right for them!

"Guys! Look out!" she shouted, and grabbed Franco's arm to pull him out of the way.

"*Ay caramba! Dios mio!*" Franco yelled as he nearly got taken out by a falling dove.

The dove landed flat on its stomach in the sand with a *thud*, and looked up at the four of them with pleading eyes. It was gasping and gulping for air. Tara fell to her knees next to the bird, grabbed her towel, and gently placed it on the ailing dove.

"You are with friends, little bird, what's the matter?"

The bird met her eyes and managed to choke out a single word before closing his eyes to rest.

Tara looked up with tears streaming down her face.

"What? What is it?" demanded Arielle.

Tara replied with the one word they dreaded.

# *"Pollution!"*

Facing the Drought

To be continued...

**THE SUPER SUSTAINABLES SONG**

**PLAY** this song at
TheSuperSustainables.com

# Water Saving Tips

# WATER SAVING TIPS 7

You can turn the faucet off when you brush your teeth. **1**

You can take 4-5 minute showers. **2**

You can make sure you don't leave faucets running and if you see any leaks at home or at school, make sure to tell your parents or your teacher so they can get them repaired right away.

You can remind your parents to do laundry only when you have a full load to wash, instead of wasting water with half loads.

You can put a bucket into the shower to collect the cold water as it warms up. Then, use this to water flowers and plants or to help your parents wash the car instead.

You can set your sprinklers to only water your yard for a short time. And if you see your neighbors using sprinklers more than twice a week, kindly remind them that 'twice is nice'.

You can be a hero too by spreading the word about how to conserve water.

# Water Saving Tips

**YOU CAN MAKE A DIFFERNCE**

Here's how much water you can save by making these simple little changes...

**If you just:** Wash only full loads of laundry and dishes
**You can save:** 50 gallons per week

**If you just:** Fix household leaks promptly
**You can save:** 20 gallons per day

**If you just:** Spend only 5 minutes in the shower
**You can save:** 8 gallons each time

**If you just:** Turn off the water while you brush your teeth
**You can save:** 2.5 gallons per minute

**If you just:** Use water-saving devices like high-efficiency toilets and washing machines
**You can save:** Many gallons per day

**If you just:** Water your lawn 1 to 2 days a week instead of 5 days a week
**You can save:** 840 gallons per week.

**If you just:** Check your sprinkler system for leaks, overspray and broken heads
**You can save:** 500 gallons per month

**If you just:** Use a broom instead of a hose to clean driveways and sidewalks
**You can save:** 150 gallons each time

**If you just:** Install a smart sprinkler controller that adjusts watering based on weather, soil type, amount of shade and plant type
**You can save:** 40 gallons per day

**If you just:** Turn off the water while you brush your teeth
**You can save:** 2.5 gallons per minute

**If you just:** Water your plants in the early morning or evening to reduce evaporation and ineffective watering due to wind
**You can save:** 25 gallons each time

For more water saving tips, visit these sites: wateruseitwisely.com and bewaterwise.com

# Water Saving Tips

Sing Along with The Super Sustainables

# Songs' Lyrics

I see the blue sky turn to gray
And wind becomes a storm
I see the climate changing
The earth is getting warm

I see the ice melting, the water rising
The tide turning, the ocean ache
I know the drought persists, I feel
land heat up
I see the crops dying
I feel the earth quake

But now I know
I hold the key
These elements, I will set them free

I will bring the elements together
Working as one, like never before
I know they'll answer my call
All for one and one for all
They're the elements
The power of four

I see the oceans polluted with trash
And smoke filling up the sky
I see oil spills dumped into the rivers
Green turns brown
And as land gets dry

Earth, water, fire and air
I have held them close to me
Now I release them
To restore the planet
To what it used to be

I will bring the elements together
Working as one, like never before
I know they'll answer my call
All for one and one for all
They're the elements
The power of four

I know the hurt you're feeling
Deep down in your core
So now I call upon a healing
I command the power of four

I will bring the elements together
Working as one, like never before
I know they'll answer my call
All for one and one for all
They're the elements
The power of four

I'm a selfie girl

Na Na Na Na Na
Na Na Na Na
Na Na Na Na Na Na

I'm a selfie girl

I'm the kind of girl who's
Always taking selfies
My friends say I obsess
And it isn't healthy
Don't care what they say
It's what I like to do
Gonna click a pic
With or without you

I'm cool at school
I'm part of the action
Texting with my friends
Is my satisfaction
Clicking, posting, liking, sharing
Having fun
Hashtag I'm number one

Check out my style
Welcome to my world
Click, post, share
I'm a selfie girl...I'm a selfie girl

Check out my dress
My hair and nails
I get my beauty on
In the tiny details
I look in the mirror, I'm all the rage
Like Katy Perry rocking
Out on the stage

Check out my style
Welcome to my world
Click, post, share
I'm a selfie girl...I'm a selfie girl

Na Na Na Na Na
Na Na Na Na
Na Na Na Na Na Na

I'm a selfie girl

Na Na Na Na Na...

Check out my style
Welcome to my world
Click, post, share
I'm a selfie girl...I'm a selfie girl

My mother says
One day when I'm grown
I can make a difference on my own
My mother says, I just have to wait
But what if by then, I am too late?

So many times adults seem unaware
The planet needs our help
But they don't care
So many times people just don't see
The future...is up to you and me

I'm praying for the earth tonight
And I pray for the power
To make it right
I wish I had the power now
To help the earth somehow

There's no time left
To wish upon a star
I think we have to start
Right where we are
There's no time left
I must find a way
To do my part and bring
A brand new day

I'm praying for the earth tonight
And I pray for the power
To make it right
I wish I had the power now
To help the earth somehow

Oh oh oh …
I wish I had the power now

Oh oh oh…
Wanna help the earth somehow

Oh oh oh …
I wish I had the power now

Oh oh oh…
Wanna help the earth somehow

Oh oh oh …
I wish I had the power now

Oh oh oh…
Wanna help the earth somehow

Oh oh oh …
I wish I had the power now

Everybody talk talk talk talk talk talk
They got nothing to say
Got my own style style
Got my own walk walk
I just turn and walk away
People wanna change me
Try to rearrange me
But they don't know a thing about me
No matter what they say
I'm gonna go my own way
Gonna be what I wanna be
So, I say

Soy soy, soy lo que soy*
I am, I am what I am
Soy soy, soy lo que soy
I am, I am what I am
Soy soy, soy lo que soy
I am, I am what I am

If there's a rule, I'm gonna break it
A risk I'm gonna take it
They say I play with fire
What you see is what you get
And no one's changed me yet
You can call me passion and desire

And you can count on me - you
know I'm gonna be
The one who always says what
he means
I live how I feel - keeping it real
I got to follow my dreams
And I say

Soy soy, soy lo que soy
I am, I am what I am
Soy soy, soy lo que soy
I am, I am what I am
Soy soy, soy lo que soy
I am, I am what I am

I am I am what I am

Soy soy, soy lo que soy
I am, I am what I am
Soy soy, soy lo que soy
I am, I am what I am
Soy soy, soy lo que soy
I am, I am what I am

*"Soy lo que soy" is Spanish for
"I am what I am"

Sitting on the beach today
If only I could sail away
I watch the tide flow in and out
I wonder what life's all about

No one seems to understand
How I feel or who I am

I know I'm different than
The other kids at school
No one seems to think I'm cool
I know being different isn't bad...
So why does it make me feel so sad?

I watch the way the water flows
Moving, steady as it goes
Every wave will run it's course
Each connected to it's source

I feel like the ocean is a part of me
I feel like a wave out there on the sea

I know I'm different than
The other kids at school
No one seems to think I'm cool
I know being different isn't bad...
So why does it make me feel so sad?

Wish I could fit in
Don't know if I can…
I'm not like the other kids
But that's just who I am

I know I'm different than
The other kids at school
No one seems to think I'm cool
I know being different isn't bad...
So why does it make me feel so sad?

TEAM SONG,

# I AM A HERO

PLAY THIS SONG AT THESUPERSUSTAINABLES.COM

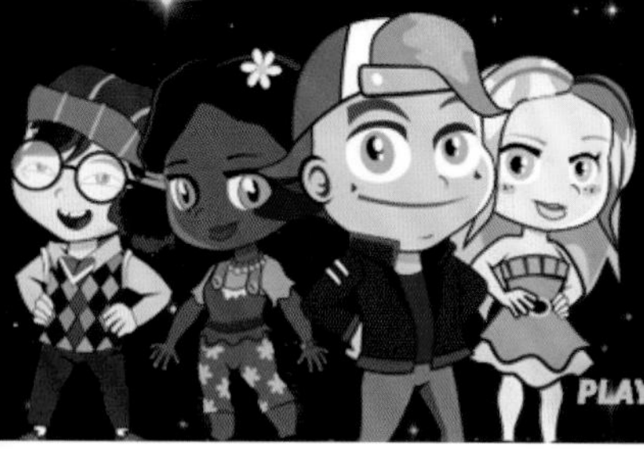

**Arielle**
I don't know what to feel
Is this all for real?

**Fuego**
It's burning my heart
I commit to do my part

**Arielle & Fuego**
Now I know I am a hero
Here today to save tomorrow

I know the earth needs me
And I know what I must do
Let's protect the earth together
Heroes, me and you

**Tara**
This feeling is so new
My dream is coming true

**Mizu**
I must protect my home
And now I'm not alone

**Tara & Mizu**
Now I know I am a hero
Here today to save tomorrow

I know the earth needs me
And I know what I must do
Let's protect the earth together
Heroes, me and you

I know the earth needs me
And I know what I must do
Let's protect the earth together
Heroes, me and you
Heroes, me and you

Mother Nature gave us life
Mother Nature gave us our home
We protect the planet
And we take care of our own

We're heroes in human form
And you can share the dream
If you're living on the planet earth
You're a part of the team

Live like a hero, like the Super
Sustainables do
Caring for the planet, yeah you
Can be a hero too

Let's all be responsible
We're the Super Sustainables
Everyone's responsible
We're the Super Sustainables
Super Sustainables

We represent the elements
United as one
We all work together
To get the job done
We are the earth, we are the water
We are the fire and wind
I hope you'll join us
Let the journey begin

Live like a hero, like the Super
Sustainables do
Caring for the planet, yeah you
Can be a hero too

Let's all be responsible
We're the Super Sustainables
Everyone's responsible
We're the Super Sustainables
Super Sustainables

Where there's pollution
We'll be there
To bring the solution
Clean water, clean air
We know that the enemy is
Indifference and apathy
It's up to you, it's up to me
To be the change we want to see

Let's all be responsible
We're the Super Sustainables
Everyone's responsible
We're the Super Sustainables
Super Sustainables
Super Sustainables
Super Sustainables
Super Sustainables

**BIG THANKS!**

To the City of Santa Monica, California and its people for creating
a foundation on which to build a sustainable future. Without your
inspiration, motivation, progressive thinking and leadership,
none of this would have been possible. May we all pull through
this drought together.

And to our incredibly generous Kickstarter backers for your
support in bringing The Super Sustainables to life. Because of
you, we are able to spread our message about saving the earth
for future generations.

**You are the real heroes!**